The Director's Cut

KRISTOPHER TRIANA

ISBN: 978-1-940250-44-1

This book is a work of fiction. Names, characters, business organizations, places, events and incidents either are the product of the author's imagination or are used fictitiously. Any resemblance to actual persons, living or dead, events or locales is entirely coincidental.

Cover Art by Lynne Hansen
www.LynneHansenArt.com

Interior Layout by Lori Michelle
www.TheAuthorsAlley.com

Printed in the United States of America

Second Edition

Visit us on the web at:
www.bloodboundbooks.net

Praise for Kristopher Triana and Body Art

"Whatever style or mode Triana is writing in, the voice matches it unfailingly . . . it's a safe bet we'll be seeing his name a lot in the years to come."

—**Cemetery Dance**

"Kristopher Triana is without question one of the very best of the new breed of horror writers."

—**Bryan Smith**,
author of *Depraved*

"Jesus! And I thought I was sick!"

—**Edward Lee**,
author of *Header*

"Kristopher Triana pens the most violent, depraved tales with the craft and care of a poet describing a sunset, only the sunset has been eviscerated, and dismembered, and it is screaming."

—**Wrath James White**,
author of *400 Days of Oppression*

"Body Art is the lost collaborative film from Larry Flynt and David Cronenberg. It's messy and brutal and a lot of goddamn fun."

—**Splatterpunk Zine**

"The most exciting and disturbing voice in extreme horror in quite some time. His stuff hurts so good."

—**Brian Keene**,
author of *The Rising*

"I've written that a way to judge the health of a genre is to gauge the number of emerging young, good writers. Kristopher Triana is one of the newest bumper crop of good ones . . . His prose is excellent, his plots compelling. Check out a rising star."

—**Gene O'Neill**,
author of *The Cal Wild Chronicles*

"Triana is a builder. He works in rural American grit, spit and the grime scraped from the windows of the soul. He uses that to build horrific and haunted adobe houses for us to cower in. He writes upon the walls and whispers in our ears, sometimes screaming when we seem too calm."

—**John Boden**,
author of *Jedi Summerr*

For Creston
My brother through all the madness

AN INTRODUCTION TO BODY ART

JOHN MCNEE

CONSIDER THE PLIGHT of the modern horror writer.

Odds are, most of the new voices to have emerged in the genre in the last decade are primarily influenced by movies, rather than literature. Sure, there might be some who insist their fascination with the horrific began when they consumed the entire works of Angela Carter and Robert W Chambers over the course of one evening when they were just three years old, but for the rest . . . it was VHS.

It's true what they all said about the video boom—the conservative campaigners, the 'family values' crusaders—about it corrupting young minds. They claimed the VHS revolution was putting the most depraved, disgusting, appalling filth into the hands of children who never should have had access to it, that exposure to these cinematic travesties was warping their fragile, under-developed brains, mangling their senses of right and wrong along with their notions of clean, Christian values.

They were right.

Reactionary, hysterical and frequently hypocritical, but they were right. Not about their predicted outcome, that it would spawn an entire generation of Satan-worshipping, mass-murdering drug addicts. That never quite happened. But as a result of the introduction of home video technology—combined with liberal or negligent parents—

children and teens growing up in the 80s and 90s had unprecedented access to an astonishing catalogue of films seething with scares, sex, and splatter never intended for their delicate eyes—including a glut of movies that previously never would have had a chance of making it into theatres.

It changed them. The impact is there to see in their art.

Without VHS we wouldn't have half the horror authors we have today.

We wouldn't have Kristopher Triana. At least, not *this* Kristopher Triana.

We wouldn't have *Body Art.*

But consider the plight of the modern horror writer.

These are people who grew up on shock and schlock, hungrily devouring the work of masters like Carpenter, Craven, Cronenberg, and Romero in tandem with B-movie heroes like Stuart Gordon and Charles Band, interspersed with the lurid foreign nightmares of Argento, Fulci, and Bava.

These were the stories they wanted to tell. Not their parents' horror fiction. Something that would distil all that they had learned about fear and depravity from this boundless cornucopia of carnage and bring it to life on the written page.

But when it came time to tell their stories, to give birth to the monstrous abominations in their heads, they found the only tool at their disposal . . . was words.

Their heroes had the benefit of special effects wizards like Tom Savini, Rob Bottin, and Rick Baker. They had atmospheric scores and engaging, soon-to-be iconic stars. And they had a thousand audio and visual tricks to manipulate their audience that authors could never hope to replicate.

An author cannot have a cat suddenly leap, screeching into the frame at a quiet moment and expect it to have the same effect as in a low-rent slasher movie. Jump scares—on which a swathe of horror movies are founded—never work in print, though there will always be those who continue to try.

Likewise, an author cannot slowly pan in on a broken tree trunk for several minutes while a discordant choir wails in the background and expect it to create tension. That technique is the sole reserve of the arthouse horror auteur who has the luxury of being able to make one paragraph on the page stretch to twenty minutes on the screen be assured of critical acclaim for their sense of slow-burning dread.

But the modern horror writer?

How can you be expected to scare people, when all you have are words?

I suppose you could, if you wanted to, abandon that aim altogether. The world of horror is littered with fantastic books that aren't the least bit frightening. They entertain, disturb, unsettle, depress—an awful lot of it is truly heart-breaking—but it doesn't *scare*. And that's fine. It is a tough ask, after all. A holdover from a bygone era when the mere suggestion of whispering figures in the mist had delicate readers soiling their nightshirts.

Horror fiction doesn't *have* to scare to be good. But when it does, is there anything better?

This is why so many continue to make it their mission, impossible as it might seem, finding their inspiration in the teachings of the old guard—King, Barker, Jackson, Poe, Stoker, all the way back—honing their craft, and boy does it take craft, to plough resolutely onward, determined that one day, however many books it may take them, through tension, shock and sheer descriptive power, they will write something that will drive the masses mad with fear.

There is honour in this, in still trying to scare people with monsters of vivid prose. And it can still work, but it relies a little too much on the sensibilities of today's horror consumers, most of whom would prefer to wait for the movie adaptation that will pep up the action with CGI, loud noises, and jump scares.

Bless the minority, incidentally, yet to be fully desensitised by the technicolor nightmare of the world around them, so that they can suspend their disbelief long enough to be genuinely frightened by a book. They are the finest people in the world.

But how do you get to the rest? And if you want to make an impact, you *must* get to the rest. The modern horror writer must find a way to reach the audience that has seen all the same films they have and, potentially, so much worse. After all, the VHS boom was immediately followed by the rise of the internet and its no-man's-land of pornography and documented atrocity.

How do you capture the imagination of someone who has had access to all that and scare them . . . with words?

Kristopher Triana has a way.

Body Art is not a book that sets out to shock—though the contents, objectively, are shocking. It is not designed to nauseate, though any right-thinking person should find the scenes depicted nauseating. But Triana's writing is calibrated not to shock, but to seduce.

There is something deeply tantalising in the sadistic, the perverse and destructive. Our society raises us to reject such deviancy. Even our art, when it explores the taboo, tends to relay it via a morally critical lens. Triana knows better than that.

The bloodlust that afflicts the sirens of *Body Art* seeps from the page to infect the readers. It coaxes them down into the warm, wet embrace of Hell and wills them to enjoy the torment. It makes sweetly-scented promises of so much worse to come and with every turn of the page it delivers. All the reader is asked to do is keep reading, keep following the spiral down—and please ignore the sound of the trap as its jaws swing shut.

In a moment of clarity—pulse racing, blood pumping, faces flush—readers may wonder why they are enjoying themselves so much.

If they can be turned on by this, how well do they really understand their own impulses? What slumbering fetish could be hidden away in the depths of their subconscious, desperate to be fed? If it awoke one day, what unspeakable horrors might they be capable of?

No man is born a monster, but as *Body Art* attests, in the right circumstances, with the right encouragement, the most innocent of creatures can be transformed into an agent of corruption.

Its exquisite trick is to turn the reader against themselves.

It scares them with the thought of what lurks within their own mind.

It beguiles and it terrifies.

To quote a brief passage from the book:

"The scary part was that Jessica had liked it.
No, that wasn't true.
She loved it."

I sincerely hope you love *Body Art.*

—John McNee

"The voyeur is impossible to satiate; he soon becomes bored by the prospects of what two people do in bed together. As experience enlarges his visual appetite, other elements have to be added in order to generate a new excitement; rape, violence, humiliation, in other words what people do to each other's bodies and to the dignity of their minds in a sexual context, so that in the end it is not the sexual act itself that the voyeur is interested in witnessing; that has ceased to be of interest way back along the voyeur's procession; that could be left for the poor sods who never got anywhere with a woman in their lives. The voyeur needs a continuation of innovative corruptions and humiliations to provide temporary satisfaction. And because the satisfaction is temporary, although the search itself corrupts completely, the search for corruption is never completed."

—Ted Lewis, *G.B.H (Grievous Bodily Harm)*

"There's something sweet you can't buy with money.
It's all you need, so believe me honey.
It ain't a crime to be good to yourself."

—Kiss, *Lick It Up*

Prologue

As he stitched Simone's arm to Tiffany's torso, he knew he was on the right track. Beauty was coming together, as were the two slabs of cold flesh. The thread danced in and out of the bloodless holes, following the stainless sheen of the pin like autumn leaves in a dust devil. Harold worked in a muse-fueled flow of unmatched speed and passion, and yet he kept his hands steady, never cheapening his craft with haste.

The ghostly pallor of their skins seemed to glow—and not just from the blue light of his studio crypt. Their illumination was due in part to the rings of light emitted by the strange, pulsating objects that floated overhead. They were like large fireflies with lens flares inside of their bellies, and they clung to the ceiling, attracted by the pungency of rot. They flew through the red dust. Harold couldn't remember when it first arrived, but the dust had become a welcomed companion, and it flurried around him now like blood snow, a tornado that fueled his depravity while also feeding off of it.

Harold breathed through his nostrils, decay kissing the back of his throat. He opened his mouth, an invitation, and tasted copper and a wisp of formaldehyde dancing in the still air.

He savored it.

Art now had a flavor.

Part One

Rated X

Chapter One

Toby had trouble watching the road. He kept staring down at her bare thighs in the passenger seat. They were long and creamy, sticking out of her jean shorts which were cut so high he could see the pockets. The pocket closest to him was fat with a bag of weed. The music was loud, the windows were down and the T-top was off, letting the warm wind of summer rip through her fiery hair.

Jessica always looked like Lindsay Lohan to him—one of his biggest celebrity crushes. She shook in her seat to the beat of Heart belting out *Wild Child,* her ample breasts jiggling beneath a Titans t-shirt.

"How much farther to the cabin?" Jessica asked.

"About thirty miles."

She put her feet up on the dash and her painted-pink toes sent his loins to stirring.

"Go faster," she said.

"Jess, I'm already doing eighty."

Toby wasn't sure what the speed limit was, but he doubted it was more than forty miles per hour. They'd made it to the rural part of the mountains and were winding through a back road. They hadn't seen another car for half an hour, and in his eagerness, he'd been pushing the old Firebird.

Toby felt Jessica's hand slide across his thigh and she moved in close, biting his earlobe. Her skin had the sweet smell of that cheap, fruity perfume she knew drove him wild. She took off her sunglasses and gave him a devilish look. Something naughty was brewing. He could see it germinating behind those green eyes.

Jessica was a little crazy sometimes. Other times, she was *a lot* crazy. That's why he found her so irresistible. Toby had been the quarterback of their high school football team over the past year and had brought them to the state championship. He knew people wondered why he'd chosen this hellcat over the head cheerleader. He could have had his pick of any girl, but Jessica was the one for him. No question. She was as red hot as her long hair and so wild she often bordered on dangerous. Now, with their senior year behind them, they were eighteen and living the high life of their final summer before he went away to college. Toby aimed to be with her as much as possible before he went off to the University of Tennessee in Knoxville while she stayed behind in Humbolt to figure out whatever it was she planned to do with her life.

"I don't know if I can wait another thirty miles." Her breath was hot in his ear and it made his neck hairs stand at attention.

"Just think about that hot tub, baby," he said, slipping his hand between those thighs.

They closed in on him like a vice, and her hand moved into his lap, rubbing the bulge taking form in his shorts. She petted his balls and then his shaft and he felt his erection struggle to move in the confines of his tight briefs.

"Let's make this ride more interesting," she said, unzipping him.

"Maybe we should wait till we get there."

"Don't be a pussy."

She pulled his cock out and unbuckled her seat belt. Then she bent over to put her head in his lap. She gave it a slow lick, then smiled up at him as she put her hand on his knee, making his foot floor the gas pedal.

"You know the rules," she said. "You can't slow down."

Chapter Two

Kandi looked in the mirror while she touched up her roots. She was a natural brunette, but the hair growing into her platinum dye-job had finally gone to gray. She'd been a blonde throughout her whole career, known for her fallow Farrah Fawcett waves, just as she'd always been known for having a black girl's ass on a white girl's body. Now that she was fifty, that ass wasn't as high and juicy as it had once been, but at least she'd never ruined her figure by having kids and still had perky tits and a smooth stomach. She had never whored herself up with implants and cheap tattoos. She'd maintained her natural, girl-next-door look even as her roles in recent films had turned her into the MILF-next-door. But that was okay. Work was work, after all, and now that she was getting on in years, said work was fewer and far between.

It wasn't like it had been when she was in her prime, back before any amateur with a video camera could slap together a skin flick and toss it up on the internet. Back in the 80s she'd thrived and had starred in more than a hundred top quality pornos between '85 and '89, including the AVN award winning films: *Blowjob Camp, Breakdance Booty, Pussy Lewis and The Screws*, and *Hard Kandi,* her first starring role. She'd been an industry star after that and had spent the following decade swimming in sex, drugs, stardom, and cash. She had spreads in *Hustler* and *Penthouse*, being the centerfolds more than once. She'd even been in a hair band's video, where she rolled around with a python and danced under hanging chains while dry-ice smoke rose around her like fog on a Scottish moor. But then as she'd entered her 40s all of that disappeared, and she found herself caving in to the changing industry. She began taking smaller paychecks from online porn sites, doing P.O.V. and shot-on-video shorts in private homes. All the stories were weak older woman fantasies—the lonely housewife across the street, the best friend's mother, the demanding boss, and similar clichés. The dialogue was improvised and the sex was directionless and routine: seduction, handjob, blowjob, straight sex, and then facial. Sometimes there was anal, but that always cost them extra.

The banality of these shoots and the uninspired schlock they resulted in always left her feeling empty and crushed by the knowledge that she just wasn't special anymore. She still had a smoking body and a pretty face, and she could fuck in ways that would make all these young punks blush. All she needed was the chance to prove herself once again by doing something fresh and original, just like she'd done in the glory days, working with other legends like Jack Cox, Bunny Hanks, and Rutger Malone. She wasn't washed up yet, was she? She wasn't too old, at least not in appearance, was she? She'd often been told she looked ten years younger than she was, and given all the spa treatments and overpriced beauty creams she threw money at, she damned well better.

With her hair bound so the dye could sink in, Kandi applied cherry lipstick and smacked her lips together. They were still plump and luscious, great cocksucking lips, and they only had the slightest wrinkles forming around them—so small that the camera wouldn't even see them with her face powdered.

Tonight she was filming another pizza-delivery man short

for a food fetish website. In a few hours she'd be fucking the "delivery boy" while he poured pasta sauce all over her and sprinkled her tits with shredded cheese. It was nonsense. It was tiresome. But it paid the bills.

She longed to find the spotlight again before it was too late. She didn't care how kinky or extreme it was, as long as it was groundbreaking and very, very good. She'd lost her inhibitions long ago as she'd tongued countless assholes and been the cum dumpster in monstrous gangbang films. She could handle hardcore. She could handle anything that was thrown her way. She was the wet dream maker, the fairy godmother of dirty sex. Nothing was taboo anymore. Nothing was off limits. No price was too high for the fame she knew she deserved.

Her phone rang, and looking down, she recognized the number from the old days. It wasn't in her contacts, but she'd punched those digits so many times in the age before cell phones that it was forever burned into her mind. It'd been ages since they spoke and she was amazed that he still had the same number. Then again, he had always been a man of peculiar habits.

"Rutger, is that you?"

"Kandi, baby," he said. "Jesus, how I've missed you and that sweet, sweet ass of yours."

"Christ, Rutger. It's been what, ten years?"

"Thirteen. Too long, darling. I want to direct you again."

Her face flushed in the mirror.

"I was just thinking about our old films," she said.

"Me too. For the last thirteen years."

They both laughed.

"Pack your bags," he said. "I'm flying you into Knoxville, first class."

Chapter Three

Harold pulled back the sheet to reveal Simone, older now and dead of course, but her face still unmistakable in its beauty. There she was, stretched out before him on one of the slabs—lips he had once kissed, eyes which had once cried over him, arms that had once enveloped his body in the soft and supple paradise that was her.

His first love: Simone Wilson. His junior high school sweetheart reduced to nothing more than just another corpse in his family's mortuary. Christ, he hadn't seen her since their senior year—twenty years ago—long after she'd dumped him. It was a small town, but he'd never seen her around—not that he went out much, of course.

Unlike the rest of the staff at Ruben's Funeral Home, Harold worked nights. He came in late to work his artistry on the dead and make them appear alive once more, however briefly, and only if an open casket was requested; otherwise he was simply in charge of embalming, a task that didn't highlight his talent. He enjoyed the night because he despised the day. There were too many people scurrying about in daylight. The nights were vacant and silent. Harold felt more comfortable with their shadows. It was an unusual practice to work the graveyard shift even as an undertaker, but Harold was an unusual man, and his older sister, Maude, had accepted this about him long ago. She owned the family business now and indulged him with these night shifts, mainly because his craftsmanship with dead flesh was simply uncanny. The steadiness of their open casket orders were due to the reputation the home had developed for making lost loved ones look positively luminous for one last goodbye kiss. Harold's gifted hands worked mortician's magic like no other.

He was more than just an undertaker; he was an artist.

Still, Harold had never worked on someone he had been in a relationship with. He thought that it might even go against a policy of some kind, like a doctor performing surgery on their son. He had not seen or spoken to Simone in decades but he recognized her the moment his overhead lamp shone down upon her. Even though she was nearing forty, her face was just as beautiful as it had been when they were young lovers. It was her best feature. He admired it now, his gaze trailing the line of her delicate jaw. Her nose curved up like a small fruit bud, and her bee-stung lips were puckered below two prominent cheekbones. Even the inevitable withering of her flesh could not detract from its delicate nature.

She was angelic.

The reality of her death stung him, as did the odd realization that came with it: he was truly alone and was running short on time. He hadn't dated in years. He'd become a hermit and a night owl, living out his years in the shadow hours while everyone else slept. His growing social anxiety had made him implode, and now he couldn't even begin to imagine having the kind of fun he'd once had with girls like Simone. Looking back on that time as he stared down at her carrion, it all seemed like some fantastic daydream. He knew, even before he embalmed her, that closing a casket on her would be closing a casket on part of himself.

"Sweet Pea," he whispered into her ear. He kissed the cold meat of her forehead and breathed in the scent of her skin.

The basement of the funeral home was his studio—a cold and metallic cellar of ambience and art. He had his disinfected hoses and tubes, his glistening stainless steel tools and the drawing boards of the long slabs. Then there were the corpses themselves; his macabre molding clay. He always enjoyed manipulating the flesh and disguising the age and disease that had brought these husks to him. He enjoyed a good challenge most of all. But Simone was hardly that. Her loveliness was a masterpiece all its own. It made him feel like a cartoonist asked to touch up Michelangelo's David.

He started with the aspirator, a medical device used to draw blood out of bodies. He inserted it into her left calf and ran the flow of blood into the hole at the foot of the slab, allowing it to fall onto the floor where it could sluice through the drain. He waited, still marveling at the fact that his first real girlfriend lay dead before him. He sighed deeply, watching her lifeblood ebb away. With the regular protocol behind him, he began dabbing at her face with powders and creams, working to highlight her features without whoring her up. Her pallor was ghostly but sensual to him. She seemed so fresh, like she'd just showered. She even smelled good.

"You'll be a special project of mine, my dear," he told her.

Running the back of his hand on her cheek, he let it fall down her elegant, swanlike neck. His fingertips grazed her collarbone, then slid down the high curve of her breast where he circled the nipple, feeling his blood flow southward. He'd never made love to her—they'd only dated for a few weeks in junior high school, having met in art class—but he'd lusted after her. But they were young. He was nervous and she was a virgin. Kissing was as far as they'd gone. He leaned down now and kissed her once again. The tip of his tongue ran across her perfect teeth and he stood up again and ran his fingers through her long, dark hair.

"I will preserve your beauty for eternity, my sweet Simone."

Chapter Four

"Don't worry, Vic. I've got a big star coming in for the next picture." Rutger spun his whiskey stones in the remaining liquid of the glass, watching them tumble and clink.

"We need it to be more interesting," Vic said. "The audience wants something more *now*. Something crazier."

"Think about it, Vic. A big starlet doing this kind of trash will really get our viewers interested. People love a fallen angel."

There was the sound of exhaled smoke on the other end of the phone. Vic always loved his Cubans.

"We'll see," Vic said. "Just don't blow the whole budget on the dame. Who is she anyway?"

"A true legend. I've worked with her before. She does excellent work."

"Yeah, yeah, yeah, but who the hell is she? We looking at a Kayden Kross or a Sunny Lane?"

"No, no. Those girls are amateurs compared to Kandi Hart."

Now the smoke was backed by a cough.

"Kandi Hart?" Vic said. "You shittin' me? She must be seventy by now. We ain't making granny porn here, Malone."

"First of all, she's only fifty and still a total babe. If you don't believe me check out her latest DVD, *Hot for Teacher VII.*

Second, she takes a dick like nobody you've ever seen. She's a true master of the cock. But best of all, she was a *huge* star, an *award-winning* star. Just imagine her doing work for us."

"You really think she'll want to do one of our films?" He paused. "Even if she does, will she keep her mouth shut?"

"She's an old friend. She can take it and she understands discretion. She appreciates it herself."

Rutger clenched his fist as he waited for Vic's reply. He knew that his last two films for Vic's special clientele had not gone over as well as he'd planned, despite how twisted and depraved they'd been. Not only did he want to work with a creative goddess like Kandi again, but he needed her—someone who could take direction and wouldn't bat an eye at the demands of a new audience.

"Okay," Vic said, letting Rutger breath again. "We'll take a shot at this. Just watch the budget. We've already dished out enough on those cameras you asked for."

"Quality tools for quality work. We can't be filming on iPhones like some frat boy."

"Yeah, yeah. Just make sure you get it shot and edited in under two weeks. And don't piss away all the cash on this has-been, *capisce*?"

"Sure thing."

Rutger knew he'd have to keep the first class ticket a secret, as well as the amount of drugs he would need to get his actors in the mood . . . if they even could get into the mood to do films like this. The last girl had quit halfway through the shoot and, once finished, her replacement said she wouldn't ever work with him again, no matter how good the coke was or how much money he offered. That was what Vic failed to understand. You either had to pay very well for this kind of performing, or you had to hire titless, herpes-infected crack whores who'd do anything for a rock. Nobody wanted to see those bony asses and yellow teeth, and he certainly didn't want to work with such human garbage.

He had standards, after all.

Chapter Five

Kandi left LAX on time and there was just a brief layover at Dallas–Fort Worth. The ride out to Rutger's ranch in the mountains didn't take long, but dusk had fallen and the day's travel had left her bone weary. Still, her excitement kept her pumped and she tried not to bite her freshly manicured fingernails. The taxi driver had chatted her up, having recognized her from her pin-up days. She enjoyed the attention, but she had trouble focusing on the conversation. She was too curious about the nature of her next film.

Rutger had been vague on the phone, but he was offering top pay for a leading role in a real film, not some cheap, online short shot on discount digital. Kandi wasn't sure what she'd be doing yet, but having worked with Rutger so many times in the past, she knew it would be something provocative and unique. He was a gifted director and a genius of perversion. In their prime, they'd made deep throat films that had put Linda Lovelace to shame and had introduced the West to *bukkake*. Rutger could take a simple bondage plot and turn it into something prodigious. His films had what all the modern ones didn't: *vision*. That was what she'd been craving, and now the thought of working again with the world's most brilliant adult film director made her salivate.

She'd hoisted her boobs into a push-up bra and showcased them in a low-cut cocktail dress, a *Rachel Pally* that she only broke out for special occasions like big auditions and dinners with executives—when she could get them. She knew her high heels would make her generous ass pop, assuring Rutger, and anyone else lucky enough to see it, that this pony still had a lot of rides left.

She lit a cigarette, knowing that the fan boy at the wheel wouldn't object to it. He would let her smoke it to a nub and put it out on his tongue if she wanted to, and hell, it wouldn't even be the first time she'd done something like that. Fans would take abuse just to have a scar that they could brag was given to them by a porn star. There had been a time when she never had to pay for food or drinks. Men had showered her with money, jewels, and cocaine. Her fame and her looks had formed an ever-flowing stream of rich benefits, and now, she hoped, she would swim in its waters once again.

She tipped the driver by putting her lipstick kiss on a napkin for him. He carried her bags to the gate where another man waited on the other side. The driver walked off, telling her that he loved her. The gate came open and a stocky man in black emerged from the shadows cast by the dogwood trees.

"Good evening, Ms. Hart." His words were wrapped in a Mexican accent.

"Hello."

As he reached for her bags, Kandi saw the tattoo sleeves running up his brown arms that tried, and failed, to cover multiple scars. He threw the bags into the back of the golf cart and took her hand to help her step into it.

"I am Javier," he said. "Welcome to Malone Ranch."

"It's been a long time."

She marveled at the bushes that lined the walkway. Each had been shaped into breasts, penises, and butts. As they drove, sensor lights came on, one by one, illuminating the genital shrubberies.

"Mr. Malone is very happy to have you back, Ms. Hart."

From the end of the driveway the giant house looked magnificent against the backdrop of a night sky. It sat in the center of the ranch, far from the stables where Rutger kept his horses. Its high pillars and arched doorways made it look like a monument. When they reached it, Javier took her hand again in a gentlemanly fashion, and then he carried her bags while guiding her up the front steps. Kandi noticed that marble statues of voluptuous women had been placed on both sides of the front doors. They were buzzed in and Javier led the way into the anteroom that opened up into the living room where Rutger stood, smiling with immaculate, bleached teeth.

"Kandi!" he said. "Come here, baby doll. Let me see you."

She moved closer, taking him in as well. He'd stayed lean even though he was almost sixty. He still had the moustache, but it had gone gray, much like his hair. He wore a red tracksuit and no shoes.

"Baby!" Rutger had her spin around. "Hot damn if you don't still got it!" he said. He grabbed her ass with both hands. "An ass like a plump Thanksgiving turkey, and twice as juicy!"

"You're looking good yourself," she said. "Very fit."

"Well, you know. The industry keeps me young. Come in, come in."

Her heels clacked on the hardwood. She remembered when it had been shag carpet. She'd done an all-girl scene there, rolling in its lush fur. She couldn't remember which picture it had been. The walls were stripped of their wood paneling now, and framed posters for Rutger's films hung on the walls. A few of them had Kandi in them, all young and firm.

They moved to the upper part of the room where a full bar was surrounded by mirrors, making the already enormous house look even bigger. During their exchange Javier made his way behind the bar and fixed Rutger a cocktail.

"Care for an Orgasm?" Rutger asked her. "It's almost as good as a real one. Amaretto, Kahlua and Bailey's Irish Cream."

She sighed at the temptation. "No thanks."

"Something else? A Long Island Iced Tea? A Blue Lagoon? Javier makes a heart stopping Bloody Aztec."

She didn't want to get into the painful story of her alcoholism and how it took David leaving her to finally get her into a program. She didn't want to tell Rutger about the DUI and the year of probation before she could get her license back; all the fees and the lawyer who'd barely helped anything, palling around with the prosecutor during breaks. She'd spent months drying out afterward, falling off the wagon, and then drying out again before she'd truly gone straight.

"I'm fine," she said.

Javier put a bottled water on the counter for her.

"Okay then," Rutger said.

They took their drinks and she followed him to the Italian sofas. Rutger's cat Cougar jumped into his lap, purring. Rutger ran his hand through her fluff.

"I saw you recently in *Hot For Teacher VII,"* he said. "You were magnificent."

"That was just a quick job. Nothing special."

"Yes, but *you* were special in it. Seducing all those schoolboys. I saw that you can still throat with the best of them. They missed out on close-ups of your signature tongue twirl though."

"The producers were amateurs."

"Clearly."

He took a long slurp from his drink and then sucked the residue from his moustache.

"Amateurs have really soiled the business, haven't they, Kandi?"

"I'm afraid so."

"They just make the same old tripe. Not an original bone

in their bodies. Not like us. We were fucking pioneers, literally. When we made *Star Whores: The Empire Spikes Crack*, we changed the game, baby."

"There was an art to it then."

"Exactly. Good porn isn't just about simple stimulation. You can get that at any titty bar. Quality adult films are about the music of the flesh, the art of the body. They have buildups that make you anticipate the action. Not like now. The actors barely say hello before they start boning. There's no character, no chemistry. People forget that the mind is the strongest erogenous zone."

"I always liked the scene in that movie *Boogie Nights*—"

"Great movie."

"Yes, that scene where the executives try to talk Burt Reynolds into using video instead of film. I love how he tells them, 'I'm a filmmaker. That's why I'll never shoot on video. If it looks like shit, smells like shit, then it must be shit.'"

"Well put! I wish I could say I still use film. I really do. But we do use high quality cameras and video—even better than DSLR, which gets blurry too easily to capture good porn. I wish film was still the standard, though. Burt Reynolds always did know his stuff. That's why he's a goddamned legend. And you are too, Kandi, baby."

She couldn't help but blush. "Well, I don't know."

"Hey now, don't give me that humble crapola. You're a star so big you're a fucking sun! You were the lead in all of my best films: *Journey to the Center of the Ass, Return of the Giving Head, A Hard Kandi Christmas*. You got those awards for a reason. Hell, you should have gotten an Oscar."

"Stop it, you'll make me blush."

They laughed and a beat of silence fell between them.

"So," she said. "You want to tell me about this new project?"

"In time. First, I just want to catch up with you. If I know my actors I can better cast them. I want the process to be organic."

"Yes, I remember. What would you like to know?"

"Shit, I dunno. Anything. Tell me what you've been doing all these years. Are you married? Do you have kids? A dog? A hamster?"

"I was married for a few years. It didn't work out. We didn't have kids because I didn't want to."

"Good for you. No wonder you look tight enough to bounce quarters off of."

"How about you?

"Yes, I married my Hannah. You may know her as Alexis Smoke."

"I've seen some of her work. She's good."

"Damn good. But our marriage wasn't. It only lasted two years. She ended up wanting kids and I didn't want to be part of that nonsense. Don't get me wrong, I don't hate children. It's just that when one of them is talking to me, I can't wait for it to be over." His face grew perplexed. "They have nothing interesting to say, and parents these days praise them so much that they're all little sociopathic narcissists. I sure as shit didn't want to have one shackled to me at all times. But Alexis did, so she left. No big deal. That's what I get for marrying a girl thirty years younger than me. But enough about me, tell me more about you."

"Not much else to divulge. Still working when I can get it, though the roles don't pay what they once did."

"Well, you won't have to worry about that with these projects. These are specialty pieces, so the pay is above average. I insisted that my backers pay a star like you top dollar."

"That's very kind of you."

"What are you used to making?"

She had once made over a grand for a male-to-female scene, twelve hundred if it included anal. But lately she'd been forced to lower her prices in the competitive market. "Well—"

"How about ten grand?"

"Ten grand?" Something trembled in the walls of her chest. "For one movie?"

"For each movie we make. The sales of the first one will dictate if there is a sequel of course, but I'm betting we'll have a smash hit."

"There must be something pretty intense for that kind of a paycheck. Are we talking triple penetration or bondage or something?"

"Perhaps, but not entirely."

"Well, you said this was a specialty project. It must be fetish then, right?"

"Oh yes, my dear. It is certainly that."

Chapter Six

Toby didn't like it when Jessica licked his anus, but that was her thing and he rarely got a warm-up blowjob without her getting in there. Jessica had some bizarre kinks and he always tried to not think about where she may have learned them. She was so good in bed and so open to try anything that he didn't complain. A little ass licking never hurt anybody.

Once she'd gotten her taste, she throated his dick and shook her head back and forth like a speed bag. When she released him, the breeze coming off the lake made her drool chill him. Before the cold could shrivel him, Jessica straddled him, pulled her bikini bottom to one side, and slid onto his cock. Unlike the other girls he had been with, Jessica never started slow. She immediately plunged him as deep into her as he would go, as if she were trying to make her womb shudder from the impact. He ran his hands up her body and she tore her bikini top away for him, letting her breasts bounce and jiggle as he pinched and slapped them.

"Yes!" she kept shouting.

He'd resisted her demand that they skinny dip. There were other cabins on this side of the lake and a ranch on the other side. He didn't want them to get caught and be thrown off the grounds on their first day.

But swimming hadn't lasted long. There was something in the water—a congealed, red allege that bobbed on the surface and gathered in fuchsia froth near the edges of the lake. Toby was concerned and they got out. But before he could investigate further, Jessica had grabbed his penis and led him to this small closure of trees.

The privacy of the trees was for Toby's peace of mind only. One of Jessica's other kinks was screwing in public. They couldn't go to the movies without her sucking him off. He had fingered her in parking lots, banged her in a department store dressing room, and gone down on her on a stack of crates behind a gas station. Every time they fucked in public, the risk of getting caught made her cum, whereas other times it was a fifty-fifty shot.

"How about Didi Harris?" Jessica asked. "How about her?"

It was a common game she liked to play while they were doing it. She would name their classmates and ask Toby if he had ever had sex with them.

"No, not her," he said.

Now came the next part of the game.

"What would you do to her if you could?" She panted. "Tell me, baby, all of it."

She'd circle through questions like these, creating fantastic orgies in her mind that involved both of them.

Toby smirked. This was one of the games he didn't mind. Jessica was more experienced than him in games of perversion, and while he winced at some of Jessica's kinks, he reveled in others. She always led him, and as long as it wasn't too fast, he didn't mind.

"I'd tear her clothes off," he said. "I mean literally tear them off—ripping and shredding them."

Jessica purred. "Then what, baby?"

"Then I'd make you go down on her, to get her warmed up for me. I'd watch for a while, then I'd have both of you fight over my cock."

Jessica writhed at his dirty talk.

She rode him for a while and just as his erection grew rock solid she got off of him and spun into the dirt so she was on her knees.

"Stick it in my ass," she said.

On top of not enjoying his own ass being violated, Toby was not a fan of anal sex. She was the only girl that had ever asked him to do it, but so far he'd denied the requests. The thought of putting any part of his body in the hole where shit came from made him want to retch.

He moved forward with his inflamed cock and dove into her flushed pussy, his breadth spreading her wide and making her cry out.

She kept groaning as she ground into his pelvis.

"Come on, baby," she cried. "Fuck my ass and you can cum inside me."

It was a tempting bonus. He always pulled out because she wasn't on birth control and they both loathed condoms. Sometimes they'd used spermicidal suppositories, but Toby didn't completely trust them, and Jessica complained about the burning sensations they gave her.

"You can cum deep inside me. Fill my ass."

But the ends didn't justify the means, so he just kept on pounding her vagina until he was about to burst. He pulled out and right on cue she slid under him so he could shoot his load all over her face, just the way she liked it. He tried to get most of it on her lips because he loved the way she would run her tongue along them, gobbling up his spunk like a kitten lapping cream. She reached for his scrotum and cupped it, letting her nails sink in just slightly.

"One day," she said. "One day I'm gonna tie you up and once you're nice and hard I'm gonna stick you right up my ass. Then you'll know what you've been missing."

They returned to the cabin, and Jessica lit some candles and put them on the deck before she threw off her bikini and climbed into the hot tub. There was a reddish pink residue on her skin, something that had gotten on her from the woods or lake probably. She splashed at it, rested the small of her back against a jet, and sunk deeper. Keeping her hands dry so she wouldn't ruin the joint, she lit it off the candle closest to her and took a long drag. She held in the smoke and passed it to Toby.

He was a great guy with a sculpted, athletic body and a slightly bigger than average penis. He treated her good, drove a fast car, and always had money to burn on fun excursions like this. Having grown up poor, she wasn't used to such luxuries. Her getaways had included dips in the public pool come summer and the occasional trip to Nashville. The only place of interest she'd ever been to had been Graceland because her mother was a hopeless, plate-collecting Elvis nut. But all of that was before Jessica was old enough to know that men would bathe young, pretty women in cash, even if there was only the slightest chance that they'd get any. She often used her body to get what she wanted. But it wasn't that way with Toby. She was happy just to fuck him in the back of his Firebird, but she certainly wasn't going to argue with a trip into the mountains or a cabin on the lake. He had a romantic heart, especially for a jock, and he often surprised her with flowers and candy. She tried to repay his kindness with surprise blowjobs, which was the one gift she could always afford.

Jessica's only complaint about Toby was that he could be a prude. He didn't even want to have anal sex, and it wasn't even *that* big of a deal. He'd cum on her face, but *all* guys like doing that, no matter what they might say. She had to beg him to slap her in the face, and when he did, it was always too soft. She wanted to *feel* it when a man took charge of her, and Toby just never had the dominance that had really made her quiver. Bruce had spoiled her with the punishment she desired. He'd taught her the joys of pain and had ruined standard sex for her. She needed something more riveting. Normal sex was adequate, but it didn't charge her motor anymore. Even a good, hard fuck just felt like foreplay to her now.

She longed for Bruce's big, black cock and hands. She was hungry for the way he'd put three of his fingers in her pussy while pumping her anus faster than most men would hit her vagina. She missed his handcuffs and his blindfolds–the way he'd sit on her face, twist her nipples and make her suck his toes clean when he was finished with her. But Bruce was a married man. He loved his wife and children. She'd known from the start that it would just be a temporary fling, and once he'd had enough of her, he moved on to another young girl. There was an endless supply of them at the high school where he taught chemistry.

It was on nights like these that she missed him the most. Toby had done his best, but she'd been dying for anal sex and he just wouldn't give in to her pleas. She tried to not let it spoil the whole night. He had rented a wonderful cabin and they didn't have a whole lot of time left to spend together. He'd be gone by August at the very latest, moving on to bigger and better things while she stayed behind in the dead dick dust of Nowhere, Tennessee. He was on to a promising football career. He may very well be the next Tom Brady.

The problem Jessica had now was her nagging resentment about Toby having a promising future that he didn't seem interested in sharing with her. She held out hope that he would still ask her to come with him to live in Knoxville. She wouldn't mind working so they could get a small but cozy apartment while he went to school. His scholarship money could go toward their place instead of a dorm. But it wasn't an option they discussed. This was Toby's big break and she would have felt bad trying to take their relationship to another level without being asked to. It was like any other kind of proposal, she thought. It was up to the man to make the first move, no matter how old-fashioned that sounded. But without Toby, her visions of the future were as devastating to her as a car crash—painful and brutal. All she was meant to be was another chain-smoking waitress or stripper with a C-section scar. She wished she had higher hopes and achievable dreams, but she had just barely graduated high school, thanks in no small part to the passing grade she'd earned outside of the classroom with her chemistry teacher. She had a lovely face and heaving breasts, while still having a trim figure. She was confident with her body more than anything else. But that could only get a girl so far for so long.

Toby kept his trunks on, stepped into the tub and sat across from her. She passed him the joint and he took a small toke. He was always worried that there would be a sudden drug test for steroids and he'd turn up with THC in his system and would be benched for the season. Toby's drug of choice was cheap beer, but they'd only brought a few and a single bottle of bourbon. He had his older brother's ID, and they looked enough alike for it to pass, but Toby was so known around their hometown that it could never work. Now that they were buried in these rural hills, they hoped they'd be able to put the license to good use.

"I wish there was a pizza place around here," he said. "I could go for a large with everything."

"You're a bottomless pit, you know that? We brought groceries. I can make some burgers when we get out."

"That sounds good."

She inhaled some more of the sweet cannabis, letting the smoke fill her lungs with the black magic that made her brain go numb and her bad thoughts fade. She only wished she had something stronger to kick off their vacation, even though she doubted Toby would partake. But the weed was giving her a nice buzz and combining its effects with that of the hot tub was making her feel quite nice. She ran her fingers through her hair and toyed with her belly ring.

"So," she said. "Who owns that McMansion?" She pointed to the ranch across the lake.

"I dunno, but they must have mega bucks."

"Might be the vacation home of a celebrity. Maybe one of the Titans."

"Could be."

"We should see if we can jump that fence and find out."

"You must be crazy. A place like that is bound to have guards."

"So. What's the worst they'll do, throw us out?"

"They'll call the cops and have us brought in for trespassing. Or worse yet we could find ourselves with a pair of Dobermans up in our asses."

At least something would be in my ass, she thought.

"We should at least give it a look before we leave."

"I brought binoculars," he said. "I always do when I'm in these mountains. I like to watch birds and animals. But you could scope out the ranch with them from right here on the deck. We've got a great view."

"I'm not getting out of this tub. You go get them."

"No way!" he said and laughed. "I just got used to the water."

"Don't be a cunt," she said, laughing now too.

He lunged at her and they began splashing, what little remained of their childlike innocence shining through.

Chapter Seven

Maude didn't notice that Simone had been one of Harold's girlfriends. It was no surprise to him. Harold had never been close to his sister and she had never taken interest in anything he did that wasn't related to the business. He found her to be dull at best and overbearing at worst. She saw him as just plain weird. She had a dumpy body and a pinched, mean face, never wearing makeup or gussying herself up with jewelry or nice clothing. She had become a spinster in her forties, and Harold believed she was a closet lesbian who couldn't face her sexuality and therefore would never be happy. The only joy she seemed to derive was from keeping their parents' funeral home running smooth and efficient after their passing. Even playing the organ at these services didn't make her smile like it once had.

The wake went well and Simone had a wonderful turnout. It made Harold feel good to know that others had loved her just as much he had. He'd made a masterpiece of her as well, just as he'd promised her he would. Everyone had commented on how beautiful she looked. He'd taken years off of her by injecting the collagen, erasing her crow's feet and the lines in her forehead. He'd given her a facial cleanse and had softened her cheeks for goodbye kisses using imported beauty creams and sugar scrubs that left her feeling softer than a newborn. Subtle touches of blush gave the illusion of flowing blood, and he'd trimmed, then stenciled over her eyebrows. He had even put her hair in curlers overnight and styled it with two different gels, blown it dry, and then sprayed it for a better shine. She probably looked more full of life lying in her casket than she had looked for the past fifteen years.

With the wake over, Harold got their hired hand Glenn to help him move her from the casket to a cot. They wheeled her through the hall to the service elevator that he used to bring the corpses to and from his basement studio.

"You sure did some nice work on this one, Harry."

"She was a special one."

"Must be all the better for you to have a clean canvas to work with."

"What do you mean?"

"She was a heart attack victim. She came to us clean. She wasn't ripped up in a car wreck or withered by cancer."

"I can make any body presentable."

"I know, but—"

"But nothing. No body is unsalvageable. Not when you're a pro."

Glenn looked away. "I'm sorry, Harry. I didn't mean no disrespect. This one just looks extra nice is all."

Glenn had been working there for almost a year now and still he hadn't gotten the hint to just leave Harold alone. He also hadn't picked up on the fact that Harold hated being called Harry. Glenn was a simple man with a simple job. He was just there to tidy up, unclog things, and help with the manual labor, such as moving bodies and making deliveries. He was not there to critique Harold's art. He was there to work.

Stupid nigger.

"Just help me get her onto the lift and then go put away all the chairs. Then get with Ms. Ruben, I'm sure she has something to keep you out of my hair."

They got the cot in and Harold closed the latch. Once down in his sanctuary, he brought Simone under the lights so he could begin prepping her for her cremation.

It was such a waste, he thought, such a shame to destroy such a fine work of art. She had always been a rather lovely woman, but now she was sublime. He had sewn her lips closed from the inside and used the needle injector to wire the jaws shut. He'd countered her sinking eyes, which had been caused by decomposition, and spent close to an hour perfecting her makeup. He had made her goddess-like in her beauty, and the thought of seeing this masterpiece consumed by flame and lost forever didn't just sadden him, it angered him. The bastards only gave her one look and then walked away. They didn't even take pictures to remember how gorgeous she was before they sent her off to be burnt down to ashes. These fools didn't appreciate what he created for them. They never did. They'd say their kind words but did nothing to really treasure what he'd done for their families. If there were any justice in the art world, everyone in attendance would be making bids as if they were at a gallery. But the art world didn't accept him as one of their own, and the people who came for these wakes didn't think of him as an artist either. He was just an undertaker, a ghoul who'd better stick to his basement full of formaldehyde and loneliness.

He caressed Simone's cheek, treasuring its velvet touch. He leaned down and inhaled her very essence. Wetting his finger with his tongue, he ran it across her lips, imagining how many lips and bodies they must have blessed. How many meals had passed through them? How many sweet nothings had they whispered? To how many men had they brought pleasure? His mind cascaded through daydreams and memoires of her, and it pained him to think he would have nothing but the photos he'd taken of her to remember her by.

She had been his first love, and now she had become his greatest work. She was someone to cherish always and something to preserve forever. To burn her up would be a crime against art and a deadly sin against beauty itself.

He took the scalpel from the tool tray and got started.

"I'm leaving!" Maude shouted from the stairs.

"Fine," he said.

It annoyed Harold when she interrupted him while he was working. It was almost as bad as when she used to just walk down and pry into his private sanctuary—that was before he'd had his tantrum and threatened to quit.

"Don't be down there all night, I don't want the electric bill to be sky high!"

"Fine."

"Don't forget to bolt the door when you leave."

"Fine!"

He'd never forgotten to lock it. Not once in twenty years. Yet she still emphasized it every night. It was enough to make his stomach acid bubble.

Hearing the front door close, he let out a sigh of relief.

Using the flexible endoscope to make sure the temporal fascia had been dissected down to the orbital rim, he cut the last bit of flesh with the skinning blade, and inserted the amino hooks, guiding them deep beneath the top layer. Deftly, and oh so carefully, he peeled it back, using the hooks to separate it from the gummy sinew. Once he freed it completely from the skull, Harold held up Simone's face in his hands and admired it. He'd thought about taking the eyes, or even the whole head, but he was never that fond of blue eyes like Simone's. He preferred his eyes soft and brown, just like the exhumed dirt of a fresh grave.

Chapter Eight

Kandi started the morning with laps in Rutger's pool and then sipped the fresh coffee Javier had made while she air-dried in the sun. He had offered to make her breakfast too, but she never ate breakfast, so she laid out poolside and let the sun's rays sink into her and massage her muscles.

She opened her eyes when a shadow fell over her.

"Good morning," the man said.

He was tall and slender, and his smile was awkward, crooked. He reached out to shake her hand. His was limp when she took it.

"Good morning," she said.

"I'm Wally. I'm your co-star."

He sat down on the lawn chair next to her. It was a warm morning, but he wore long pants and a flannel shirt.

"Nice to meet you, Wally."

"I'm really excited. Are you excited?"

"I'd say I'm more curious. Do you know what we'll be doing?"

"Oh, I wouldn't want to spoil the surprise. Mr. Malone always wants reactions to be genuine."

"I'm going to need some sort of direction if he expects me to get this right." She leaned forward, turned on her charm. "You sound like you know something that I don't, Wally."

He scratched at his bald spot and stared off into the blue swirl of the pool.

"Don't worry. It'll all make sense."

"Okay," she said, giving up. She could wait.

"This is a big day for me."

Kandi tried to stay polite, but she'd grown tired of him already. Just 'cause she may have to fuck him later didn't mean she had to listen to him. "Oh yeah?" she asked. "What makes it so big?"

"It's my first porno shoot."

She sat up and took off her sunglasses.

"What?"

She looked at Wally. He was freakishly tall, so maybe he had an anaconda for a cock, but other than that he was nothing to look at. He was at least in his forties, pasty, and had pockmarks in his sallow cheeks. If he had been a former star she could have understood. But this guy said he was an amateur, the very type of people she had grown so sick of working with. She was surprised at Rutger. After their talk last night, she expected to be making something more upscale. She couldn't believe what she was hearing.

"You've never been in a porno before?" she asked.

"No."

"Well that's just fucking perfect."

"Excuse me?"

"You don't know what you're doing. The shoots will take twice as long because of that. The quality of the whole film is going to suffer, whatever the fuck it's going to be. No offense but it takes talent to make a good porno. You have to know what you're doing."

"Don't worry, baby," Rutger said.

He approached them with Javier close behind, carrying a tray of Bloody Marys.

"You mind explaining this to me?" Kandi pointed to Wally with her sunglasses.

Rutger sat down next to her, took his drink, and swirled the celery stick coyly.

"Wally won't ruin a thing. He has only one scene, no lines, and he'll be strapped down through the whole thing."

That made her feel better, but it also brought up more questions.

"How long can he last without cumming?" She asked the question without so much as a glance at Wally. "He won't cum inside me and blow the money shot will he?"

"Oh, honey, you won't be fucking him," Rutger said. "You know I always give you options. I let you have the stud of your choosing. You don't even have to blow him."

Rutger took the celery stick and put it into his mouth, sucking the grinds of pepper off of it. He took a second drink from the tray and handed it to Kandi. She looked at it for a moment, then passed it over to Wally. He drank it immediately.

"When are you going to fill me in?" she asked.

"It has to be fresh, darling. You know how I work. I give you the instruction the moment before the camera turns on. It has to flow naturally to capture the magic of real eroticism."

"I know, and I respect that. It's made for excellent work in the past. But I at least knew what kind of sex it would be and how many people would be in the scene. I had lines I had to remember. I need to be ready."

"There's no way you can prepare for this. You'll just have to roll with it, baby. Don't worry. Have I ever let you down before?"

The room was cold—colder than normal for a porn shoot. Kandi understood if Rutger wanted her nipples to pop, but she felt like she might start shaking once she took off the kimono, which was all she had on. In the center of the room was a metal slab and lying there was Wally, naked. His legs and his right arm were strapped to the slab, but his left arm was free. He looked asleep. Beside the slab was an elevated chair with two stirrups sticking out of its base, the same kind used by her gynecologist. On the other side was a small rolling table.

The light check was done and now the boom operator, Mia, the only other woman in the room, was positioning herself. The two cameramen, Tye and Ben, were behind their lenses, and Rutger sat in his director's chair, twirling an unlit cigar as he watched her, even though she wasn't doing anything yet. Finally, he spoke.

"How're you feeling?"

"Okay," Kandi said. "A little chilly."

"Sorry. It has to be cold for this."

"All right."

"I want you to know that you're in good hands. You know I take good care of you, right, baby?"

"You always have, Rutger."

"Right. I would never put you in a bad situation. Remember that."

He was confusing her now, even scaring her a little. But she did trust him. He'd never given her a reason not to. He'd always been straight with her and had never told her lies. Never ripped her off for her work or released a movie they'd made unless he felt it was absolutely perfect.

"Don't worry about Wally," he said. "He's making good money today. He's consented—signed the forms. He's here because he wants to be here."

"Are you going to give me direction now?"

"Yes. When you're ready, take off your kimono and get into the chair. Recline and put your legs into the stirrups and turn toward the camera so we can see your pussy. The others will do the rest. You just watch Wally and what the others do to him and masturbate. All you do here is pleasure yourself.

No one is going to touch you and you're not going to touch anyone. Just *do not stop* masturbating. I can't stress that enough. We have to get this in one take."

"How do you want me to masturbate? Rub my clit, or finger myself or . . . "

"Whatever makes you feel best. Try and make yourself cum."

She disrobed and got into the chair. The stirrups spread her wide. Another man came into the room wearing a long, white coat over a rubber apron. He carried a black bag and wore workman goggles strapped to his shaved head. He paid no attention to Kandi and placed his bag on the table next to where Wally lay. Wally looked up, groggy but awake. He smiled, seeing her spread legs and freshly waxed pussy on display.

"Rolling," Tye said.

Ben snapped a clapperboard in front of Tye's camera and said: "Untitled 7, take one."

"And the only take," Rutger said. "Action!"

Kandi looked into the camera and wet her fingers, then rubbed her clit in a circular motion, massaging her breasts using the other hand. Wally watched, using his free hand to play with himself. Kandi saw Rutger nod with approval, then turn to the man in the coat and give him a hand signal. The man smiled at the camera. Without saying a word, he opened the bag and pulled tools out of it. Looking at them, Kandi was reminded of surgical implements.

A doctor flick . . . Pretty standard.

Among the tools were scissors, scalpels, and one that looked almost like a big hair curler. Kandi continued to play with herself, though there wasn't much to stimulate her other than the rolling cameras. But she'd worked her way through countless scenes that she just wasn't into. It was just part of the job. She began moaning, trying to make it more exciting for her, hoping she could make it if she just faked it for a while.

Wally, however, was very into it. His erection was long in his hand and he jerked it rapidly, ferocious, as if he wanted to rip it from his body. He didn't seem to care or even notice when the doctor stuck him with a syringe. He just kept on jerking as he stared at Kandi's wet vagina. They both masturbated for a while as the doctor sorted his tools. Then the doctor lifted a scalpel from his tray and took hold of Wally's arm.

What the hell is this? Not a cutter fantasy. Come on.

She tried not to glower as she kept rubbing her clit, watching the doctor make a clean cut all the way around Wally's bicep. Wally seemed more than okay with it. Already the head of his penis was swelling. Once finished with the incision, the doctor tied a thick rubber band around Wally's arm, just above the cut. Then he put the goggles over his eyes and lifted an electric tool that had a small, circular saw blade. Kandi turned from the camera and looked at Rutger.

What is this?

Rutger pointed at the chair, signaling her to lay back and reminding her not to stop. She did and continued to finger herself, watching as the doctor brought the blade to life, spinning with a menacing whir. Wally smiled at the sound and she saw a bit of pre-cum dribble out of his dickhole. The doctor leaned down, and with a gentle swoop, he sent the saw into the cut on Wally's arm. Blood splattered on the doctor's apron and across his face. It sprayed up onto Wally's neck and splashed his lips. He lapped at it in dog-like slurps. Kandi was mortified and yet she couldn't look away, the whole time still working her pussy. This wasn't just a quick incision for a spatter effect. The doctor was grinding the blade down against the bone, creating a sickening, wet sound. Somehow Wally kept jerking off. He moaned louder and louder. His feet shook in their shackles and his eyes rolled into his skull.

Rutger's words from earlier ripped through her mind.

Don't worry about Wally. He has consented. He's here because he wants to be here.

The blood was pooling under Wally's back and dripping onto the floor. He arched, squealed, and thrust his pelvis out as he came. His hand fell limp beside his spouting cock, which flopped freely, filling the air with ropes of jizzum. He passed out and Kandi watched as the doctor spun the blade deeper through the meat and sinew until she heard it hit the metal slab. He put down the blade and took Wally's arm, pulling it up and tearing away the remaining fleshy strings that held the appendage to his body. He placed it on the rolling tray and lifted the hair curler, which she now realized was a huge soldering iron. It was glowing bright now and the doctor put it to Wally's stump, cauterizing the wound. The stink of burning flesh filled Kandi's nose as one camera zoomed in on the stump and the other zoomed in on her. Being a pro, she put on her best horny-slut face and screamed as she forced herself to climax.

"And cut!"

Rutger stood and applauded while the others scrambled to get the equipment away from the blood spreading across the floor. The boom operator opened the door and stepped out; her face had gone pale. Javier came in with a mop and bucket. Kandi got out of the chair. She wrapped herself in the kimono, and Rutger put his hands on her shoulders and kissed her on the cheek.

"Beautiful!" he said. "The expressions on your face, the way you used your fingers, and the way you didn't turn away from what you saw. You are a true professional."

Another man had entered and he and the doctor undid the locks on the slab's legs and wheeled Wally out of the room.

"This is going to be our most groundbreaking work yet," Rutger said. "And it's all thanks to you, Kandi. You're my shining star!"

She took a deep breath, watching Javier sopping up the

blood and draining it into the bucket. She returned her attention to Rutger.

"We need to talk," she said.

"Apotemnophilia," Rutger said. "That's what they call it."

They were in his den. Rutger was sipping a White Russian and petting his fat cat, who purred in his lap with half-closed eyes. Kandi was sitting across from him. She had showered and dressed, and her troubled look intensified by lack of makeup. Rutger understood how she must feel. It had been quite an adjustment for him, too, when he'd first started making these films. Over time he had grown immune to most shocks, but even he became a little squeamish when it came to dismemberment porn.

"It's a particular fetish," he said. "Sexual arousal caused by envisioning yourself as an amputee. It's commonly associated with Body Integrity Disorder—which our friend Wally has. People with this affliction are otherwise perfectly sane, but they obsess over the desire to remove a limb from their bodies. This is different from people who simply want to have sex with an amputee. These people want to become one themselves."

Kandi sat with her hands crushed between her legs, looking like a nervous little girl about to be disciplined. Rutger wished he had a camera on her.

"So Wally wanted this?" she said.

"With his whole heart. He also got paid very well for his performance today. It was a double win for him."

"He could have died."

"That is a risk. But this is a risky business. He was taken to a special clinic immediately after. He's expected to be okay."

"Is that what the doctor said?"

"What doctor?"

"Jesus!"

"You mean the man who operated? He's a medical student. The work he does for us is paying his tuition. Plus he gets a lot of practice."

"This can't be legal."

"Well, the surgery isn't, but Wally signs a waiver and consents on video."

"But how can you possibly distribute something like this?"

"I leave that to my producer. He has contacts across the globe for these specialty films. They're mostly sold to foreign markets but we have select fans here in the States."

"So it's all underground."

"Of course. Entirely."

Kandi sighed. "I thought you were going to make me a star again."

"Oh, but I am. To a whole new audience."

"But what if one of these movies comes to the surface? I don't want to be an accessory to a crime."

He stood up and walked around the desk to her, putting his hands on her shoulders. "Kandi, honey, as I said before, this is a risky business. We put our names, faces, and bodies out there for the world to see, and once you're out there you can never leave. You're a porn star for life . . . even after you quit making films. You lose your humanity among normal people. We both know that. You're recognized wherever you go. That's a sacrifice.

"Those who make porn are like martyrs. We create sex for those who can't get it themselves; those who don't want to cheat on their wives but are secretly bored with them; the nymphomaniacs and the strip club junkies. We get them off and what do they do in return? They frown upon us. They see us as peddlers of filth even though they are our customers."

"But what does that have to do with making illegal porn?"

"Everything, baby. We're already seen as scum, as

monsters. So we've got nothing to lose and everything to gain. The amateurs have stolen our art from us. They've taken our rightful paychecks away. So, we turn to the black market. We do what the amateurs can't. We break the mold once again, Kandi, and in doing so, we become immortal."

Chapter Nine

In this small way Simone would live forever.

Harold kept her face floating in the jar. He wrapped up her severed arms in shrink wrap and folded them so they would fit in the freezer, sticking them under his frozen pizzas and strawberry shortcake bars. The arms were so lovely and toned. She'd gained no dangling flab. But it was the hands he was most attracted to—the first hands, other than his own, that had ever touched his penis.

It had been through his jeans, but she had grabbed it just the same and had rubbed on it for a minute until he'd came, flooding his underwear. She had giggled at how quick he climaxed and he'd blushed with shame. It was decades ago, but the sting of that giggle still sent needles through him. Despite that, her quick handjob had been his first sexual encounter, and he felt like it was worth keeping a memento.

Simone was something special. She marked something Harold could not yet identify but felt pulsing under his flesh. But collecting body parts was not new to Harold. He had a private collection of eyeballs, fingers, toes, nipples, clitoral hoods, and slivers of labia. He only collected what he considered prime cuts, and he kept them locked in the basement's freezer, away from his sister's prying eyes.

All of the parts were from women because his collection was sensual to him, and the thought of preserving male body parts repulsed him, much as gay sex would. He loathed homosexuals. He thought of them as diseased fags and sodomites, and found the male body sickening overall; the dead worm cocks and hairy turkey giblets; the furry arms, legs, and asses; the beer-swollen bellies and bacteria-collecting moustaches. He couldn't even understand why men were attractive to women, let alone another man. The thought not only astounded him, it enraged him.

He heard a throbbing noise coming from the street above and realized it was bass coming from woofers.

Yet another nigger blasting that rap crap. When they're not hooting through a basketball game, they're making the rest of us listen to their shitty music.

The sound grew louder and then faded away as the car drove past.

God forbid they just enjoy the silent serenity of a summer night, or have a single moment of quiet contemplation. No. They'd rather fill their empty heads with noise made by equally empty heads.

There ought to be a law. Had I been working, my hand could have slipped.

During the colder months Harold was able to make the pickups after dark, which he preferred. But now it was light outside until almost nine and he had to get to the flower shop before they closed at seven. The wreaths that Maude had ordered were ready and they would need them by tomorrow morning.

As much as he loathed going out in public, he did enjoy seeing Tiffany.

She was the head florist at the shop and she was very

friendly to him, despite his awkwardness. She had a sunny aura that lulled him like a child into its mother arms. She had perfect teeth, deep brown eyes, and long legs that he often dreamed of being wrapped around him. She was in her late twenties and her skin was smooth and tan from days spent in the summer sun. Her vibe was one of jubilance and carefree happiness, the kind of happiness Harold had never really known, and he envied her youth and sheer ability to just relax and have fun.

He came in with his head tucked into his shoulders like a school boy with a crush on his teacher.

"Hello, Tiffany."

"Hey you," she said. "I'll go get them. Be right back."

He tried to smile and hoped it didn't come off as a morbid grimace, the rictus of a corpse in rigor mortis. She went into the cooler and came back out with the plastic-wrapped wreaths. Totaling it up, she took his money and gave him change.

"Business good?" she asked.

"Yes. Very good."

It seemed awkward to say so. His business profited over death and grief. At least her business profited off of a combination of love and death, a mixture he much preferred.

"How's business for you?" he asked.

"Doing okay, I guess. I don't keep track of the books, but I've been making a lot of bouquets. I guess love is in the air now that the sun is shining again."

He felt his index finger picking at his thumbnail, a nervous habit.

As a young man he would have asked her out by now. He didn't know where his confidence had gone, but he figured he had lost it somewhere in the dark belly of that basement. He'd lost his sense of life by living with the dead. When he looked in the mirror he no longer saw a man, but a ghoul. Sure, he was ten years older than her, but that wasn't his main deterrent. It was his crippling doubt of his humanity.

"Will that be all?" she asked.

I'm afraid so, he thought.

With Simone's ashes in the receptacle, Harold washed his hands and put on fresh gloves to work on the elderly woman who had arrived earlier in the day. He let her blood drain while he prepared the formaldehyde and tools, listening to Wagner and sipping on a cheap chardonnay as he worked.

When the buzzer rang, he winced at the interruption. He went to the transmitter and pressed the button.

"What is it? I'm working!"

"Got another one for you," Glenn said.

"Fine."

The elevator came down and Glenn pushed the cot out. A white sheet covered the body, but Harold could tell it was a female by the large breasts that indented it. Glenn wheeled her over the drains next to the old woman.

"Anything else?" Harold asked.

"Maude asked me to get the urn. Is it ready?"

"Of course it is."

Harold gave it to him and Glenn turned and got into the elevator without another word, and for that Harold was grateful. He listened to it rise, heard the door, and listened to Glenn's footsteps above, making sure he was alone.

He downed the rest of his wine and stepped toward the new body. He raised the bottom of the sheet first, slowly, letting the fabric reveal tan thighs. The vagina was shaved, like it had been taken care of just before her death. Its lips were already turning purple. He pulled the sheet higher and saw the torso wrinkled from childbirth, and heavy, fake breasts. The nipples had been cut to insert the silicone, leaving scars that made them look like octagons.

Fucking novices.

He gave the breasts a good squeeze, having never felt fake ones before. They had no give to them, no bounce, and he didn't like them at all. He felt it was foolish for man to believe flesh could be imitated. Plastic mixed with human tissue was a hellish synergy, disrespectful and wrong.

Breasts should feel like pillows, not basketballs.

He drew back the sheet completely and tossed it on the table. When he turned back to the corpse he saw her face, and at first he didn't recognize her. She'd had her lips plumped since he'd last seen her and she'd had at least one face lift. He may not have recognized her at all if it hadn't been for her eyes. He had never forgotten those eyes, and he knew he never would. They were a chocolate brown with tiny rivers of lime pointing toward the pupils. They were wide and staring now, just as they had been when he'd first made love to her.

He stumbled backward, overturning his workstation. Falling to the floor he scooted back against the wall, shuddering. Feelings of fear and paranoid rage coursed through him and he began searching the corners of the ceiling for hidden cameras, but he saw only concrete and pockets of what looked like reddish mold that had formed in the cracks.

Is this some kind of game?

He stood back up and went to her again, just to be sure. But there could be no doubt. Even with all of her surgeries, he could see that it was she. He swallowed hard and tried to keep his hands from shaking. Sweat beaded at the small of his back and he began to chew the inside of his cheeks.

Carrie. Dear God, two in one week. It has to be more than a coincidence.

She had no wounds. She did not appear to have been in an accident, nor had she been murdered or committed suicide, unless she'd overdosed or ingested poison. She was still young, only in her late 30s. He ran his fingers through her dark curls and leaned into her.

"Why are you all coming back to me now?"

She had been his second serious girlfriend. They'd attended the same art school and in the second year of their relationship they had moved in together. She was a sculptor, though not a good one in his opinion, and she earned extra money as a nude model. She'd had a striking figure then—full breasts, long legs, and hair that went all the way down to her knees. They'd been together for three years before she cheated on him with a gymnast, a black man.

"First Simone, and now you."

His paranoia blossomed. He wondered if someone was killing off his ex-lovers in an attempt to frame or blackmail him. He didn't think he had enemies, but he was unabashed in his misanthropy and could have easily upset someone. Perhaps he had done a job on someone's dead mother that they did not approve of. Maybe the home had overcharged a client or had somehow bumbled the services. He couldn't think of any such error, but perhaps the customer had remained silent in their fury and made a vow of creative retaliation.

Then again, it may not have anything to do with revenge. There may be no assailant lurking in the bushes, bumping off his former girlfriends and watching him as he became unglued. It could just be a coincidence.

Or it could be fate.

He had been lonely. He had longed for a woman's touch. These feelings had got him thinking about better days; reminiscing about old flames and the tenderness he'd shared with them that seemed entirely alien to him now. Was it possible that destiny had reunited him with these lovers as a way to help him rekindle his sour heart? Maybe it had. Maybe this homage to unrequited love was a sort of blessing. It gave him a chance to reconnect with these women and, in turn, remember what he'd been that had made them love him. There was no longer any distance between them. The arch of time had come full circle and they were once again before him, awaiting his loving touch.

There were no barriers anymore, no boundaries.

The only divider was the line between life and death, and it hovered there in the dim light of his sanctuary, as if begging to be violated.

Chapter Ten

That afternoon Kandi sat in her room and watched the videos Rutger had given her. She wasn't sure what he expected to achieve by doing so, but he insisted that she take a look before deciding if she wanted to continue.

The tapes were intense.

In fact, they were downright crazy.

Silicone bimbos punching a smiling clown in the face and then peeing on him as he lay unconscious on the floor; a girl having sex with ventriloquist dummies that shot yogurt from their wooden boners; three men having an orgy in a pool full of manure and cow's blood. But the tapes got progressively worse. Soon she was watching women bent over filthy bourbon barrels while they were whipped with barb wire; men having their chests grated by dominating Amazons; a man shaving a thin layer of flesh off of another man's penis and giving him a blowjob of blood; another man having his balls kicked around by midgets; a woman having her nipples torn off by hooks attached to a truck's bumper.

Those were the videos that intrigued her the most. They were intense, provocative. As horrific as they were, they were also completely engrossing. Each held the style that was uniquely Rutger Malone's. The gorgeous cinematography—

Rutger would film an actor's face in the moment of sexual bliss in the same way most filmmakers would shoot landscapes—his taut pacing that left you hungry for the next frame, Rutger bringing out the very best in his performers, and, most of all, how he managed to capture unbridled emotion and feed it back to the viewer.

He was the Shakespeare of smut.

These gory sex tapes had stunning power. They grabbed the viewer and spread their eyelids as far as they could go. In a weird way, Rutger was right. These were a new form of art. Some art was meant to shock. It was supposed to make people feel things they'd never felt before. These tapes did exactly that. There was nothing banal about them. They were tantalizing, electric, and entirely original.

Kandi had grown so used to making the standard trash, she'd almost forgotten the raw power that sex on film could possess. And perhaps most viewers of pornography had grown desensitized to it too. The world needed porn like this. It shattered all perceptions of voyeurism and pulled the viewer so far in, that they themselves felt like a part of the film. And because the movies were deep underground, the viewers truly were part of the art itself. There was no way to watch them and not *feel*.

This was how these films brought pornography back to its purest and most admirable form. It was the documentation of humanity, primal and pitch-black as it may be.

"I'm so glad you've seen the light," Rutger said.

They were sitting out on his deck over the lake. Rutger was puffing on a cigar and swishing his bourbon. The sun was high in the cloudless sky and the maple trees made soft shadows on the rippling water. Kandi was back in her bikini, bathing in the rays.

"Where do we go from here?" she asked.

"We're filming again tonight. Take a look at these." He handed her pictures of three naked men. "Tell me which one you want to fuck."

"Just one?"

"For this scene, yes."

They were all muscular and chiseled with perfect hair and teeth. They were young, handsome, virtually indistinguishable, like clones popped out of a stud vending machine. She wasn't pulled toward any particular one. When she'd been young and new in the game, Kandi enjoyed picking her sex partners based on looks alone. She'd gotten off on it. But as she'd matured, the decision came down to ones she'd had good experiences with in the past, ones she got along with, or, if they were all new to her, whoever looked the cleanest.

Kandi shrugged. "I'll take whichever one is going to put on the best show."

"That would be Billy Zap." He pointed to the blonde. "He can get hard from a slight breeze and keep it that way for hours. His dickhole's like the Hoover Dam . . . but once he lets it go, you'd better brace yourself. It's like a fire hydrant. He'll be fucking you and a girl called Diamond Detroit. She's done a lot of quality work for me. The two of you will go at it too. Basic threesome."

"I don't suppose I get to know what the twist is."

"Nope."

"Let me be clear: I don't want to be hurt."

"I wouldn't dream of seeing an impeccable body like yours injured, Kandi."

He turned to her, grinned wide enough to show his gold tooth, and slammed back the rest of his whiskey. Kandi got up and removed her top, letting her pale tits get some sunshine. She sat on the edge of the dock and let her feet sink into the lake. The water was mild, and she flashed back to her honeymoon with David in the Bahamas and the romantic nights they'd shared upon the shore that sparkled beneath a swollen moon like tinsel. It seemed that everything reminded her of him lately. He was a ghost she couldn't shake, and, deep down, she didn't really want to. Better to have a fading memory of him than to not have him at all.

She'd had sex with roughly two thousand men, but David had been the only one she'd ever made love to. He was the only man who wasn't threatened by her profession, who understood that it was a job and nothing more. He was adoring and understanding, even as her drinking problem had escalated. He'd tried to get her to stop. He'd made it so she had to hide the wine bottles in the house. Eventually it came to a point where he'd accepted that she wasn't going to quit. All he had asked was that she left the drinking to when she was at home. He just wanted her to be safe; to not hurt anyone, including herself. But she hadn't even been able to keep that promise. When the BMW got totaled, it was the final push that sent David out of her arms for good.

"I'm going to head in," Rutger said. "Javier can fix you something before the next shoot. We'll start in two hours."

"Sounds good." She kicked at the water, making the memory ripple and fade into the murk.

Chapter Eleven

The woman was standing on the deck across the lake—topless, stretching. Toby watched through the binoculars, and the excellence of her figure combined with the sheer voyeurism of it made his pants tighten. Jessica was still showering after their hike, and he had been bird-watching, hoping to catch a glimpse of a red-shouldered hawk or a yellow-billed cuckoo or any of the other birds native to the area. But instead he'd found this gorgeous woman and his fetish for women old enough to be his mother kicked in.

He adjusted the binoculars, zooming in as the woman turned around. When he saw her face, he blinked hard, thinking the sun was playing tricks on his vision.

Holy shit-snacks. That's Kandi fucking Hart!

There was no mistaking her. Toby owned several of her classics on DVD and regularly masturbated to her newer videos on the net. He subscribed to *MILF Magnet* and *Hungry, Hungry Housewives*. It wasn't that he didn't enjoy the young, taut flesh of girls his own age, but something about an older woman succumbing to him made his motor smoke, and while he'd never had sex with an older woman it was a reoccurring fantasy. He was nuts about Nina Hartley, Jodi West, and Darla Crane, but Kandi Hart was his absolute favorite. His father's worn and static-filled VHS copy of her 1983 masterpiece, *Cum on Feel the Boyz*, had been the first porno he'd ever seen. He was thirteen then and had been hooked on her ever since, hunting down her old boner-jams and snatching up her magazine spreads on eBay.

He watched as she jumped into the lake. When she surfaced, her breasts bounced, and Toby licked his lips at the water rolling down her body. With her hair wet and slicked back, he could see her face more clearly. She was exquisite in the sunshine; a beauty born and a body made for sex. She was well over forty now, but she looked better than most of the girls from school. In many ways he even thought Jessica, cock-pudding that she was, might pale in comparison.

"Who's the babe?"

Jessica had stepped up behind him and was standing there, also wet and topless.

It was a dead heat.

"She's a porn star," Toby said.

"Seriously? How can you tell?"

"I recognize her. She's really famous. Her name is Kandi Hart."

"No shit? She's really a porn star? Are you sure it's her?"

"I'd know her anywhere."

"Oh yeah? She a favorite of yours?"

"Fuck yeah. Hands down."

Jessica chuckled and moved in front of him. She knelt down and started to unbuckle his jeans.

"What are you doing down there?" he teased.

"You just keep watching the queen."

She put him into her mouth and rolled her tongue, then started jerking him off.

"This is so hot, baby," she said.

He kept his hands on the binoculars, watching Kandi swim and tumble, her body like milk in the twinkling basin. Jessica stood, then sat in his lap, sliding him into her wet pussy. She bent forward so Toby could still get a good view. He noticed that Jessica was watching her too.

"She might not be making a porno over there," Toby said. "I mean, this is a vacation spot. Maybe that's her summer home or she's visiting a friend or something."

"But maybe not," Jessica said. "We could be right across the lake from a real porn shoot. How cool would that be?"

"Pretty cool. But we can't be sure."

"But we can find out for sure."

Jessica got that mischievous look in her eye and bit her bottom lip. This was an exciting addition to their little fiesta, and she wasn't about to let him just shrug it off like they were deciding what shoes to buy.

"We could get in big trouble," he said. "Famous people have bodyguards and good lawyers. I doubt they like fans climbing their fence."

"That's half the thrill, baby. Just the thought of sneaking around that ranch and peeping in the windows gets me all juicy."

She rubbed his thigh and uncrossed her legs. She was wearing only a pink wife-beater that said *Rebel* across her breasts and a matching thong. She leaned back further and showed him how moist she'd grown.

"How much do you like porno?" she asked.

"As much as any other guy. But I'm not obsessed with it or anything."

"But you *are* obsessed with this Kandi woman."

"She's just my favorite is all."

"Girls like porn too, you know. Guys think we don't, but we do. I watch it. It gives me good ideas."

"Now *that* I believe."

"Can you imagine having sex with so many people that you lose count? Fucking in front of a camera, knowing thousands of people are going to get off on you doing it with a stranger. It'd be like winning the lottery."

"You want to make porn? We've done that already."

"Don't you dare compare home movies to what that woman across the lake makes. You might as well compare Kanye West to Beethoven."

Toby blinked, his mouth slack. "You're serious, aren't you? You'd really like to be in porn?"

"Sure, why not?"

"Is that why you want to go over there, to ask Kandi for a job? I don't think that's how it works, Jess."

"I just want a taste." She crossed her legs back and moved closer to him. "I want to see her in action, up close. I want to feel the heat and smell the sweat and cum. It's got to be so much more than sex. It's got to be like a fever dream."

She started rubbing his crotch and he shifted away from her.

"I think he's down for the day," he said.

She held back a sigh.

She'd yet to find a man who could keep up with her.

They crept through the grass around the edge of the property. They didn't want to bring flashlights, so they stumbled under a moonless sky. The night wind had come and it blew coolly across their bodies, chilling the sweat that beaded at his brow.

How did I let her talk me into this?

His nerves rattled his bones and he tried to keep from shaking as they approached the fence. If Jessica caught him trembling there would be no end to the mockery. He tried to remind himself that what they were doing wasn't that big of a deal. It wasn't like they were going to break in or loot the place. They were just trying to catch a glimpse of what Jessica hoped might be a porno set.

Toby just wanted a better look at Kandi Hart. He found

himself wishing he'd brought along the 1985 Penthouse that she had been the centerfold in. If he saw her down by the lake again he could have asked her to sign it.

The gate was made of iron bars and had gold letters at the latch: RM. Toby figured then that it wasn't her house. Looking at the tall bars reaching up into the dark, he wondered just how the hell Jessica thought they'd be able to scale the damned thing. In a way, he was relieved to see how daunting it was. It meant it would be easier for him to talk her out of this nonsense.

"I don't think we can get over this gate," he said.

"You can hoist me up. If I stand on your shoulders, I'll be able to swing over it. Once I'm on the other side, I can open the gate for you."

"Christ, Jess. Just give it up. You'll break a leg doing this."

"Come on, we've come this far. Don't chicken out on me now."

She knew his weak spot. He hated being called a coward.

"This is stupid," he said, but he knelt down anyway and let her climb onto his back.

She used the bars for balance as he rose up and she stood upon his shoulders. She had to stretch to get her hands on the top of the fence, and she had to jump off of him to grab hold. But she made it. He doubted she would have the upper body strength to pull herself over, but she was a determined girl and her hardheadedness gave her uncommon power. She straddled the top in triumph and then slid over and dangled from the other side. Then she let go, tucking and rolling into the bushes.

"Piece of cake," she said.

She went to the front of the gate where the latch was and paused.

"Shit," she said. "It's locked."

"Well, yeah, so unlock it."

"No, dummy, I mean it's locked from this side. It needs a key to open."

"Shit!"

"Calm down, Toby."

"Don't you realize what this means? The whole place is gated. That means you're stuck in there. You can't scale the gate by yourself."

He watched her excited expression turn to dread as she realized he'd been right.This was a bad idea.

"Goddamn it, Jess!"

He shoved the gate and it clamored.

"Chill out," she said. "Don't make it worse by making noise."

"What are we gonna do?"

"I don't know. We'll figure something out. Maybe I can find something to climb on."

She turned and they both looked at the manor and around the long stretch of property. In the distance a horse was wandering in a small enclosure near the stables and track.

"Maybe I can get up on one of those horses. They look big."

"Are you insane?"

"They're all trained. Just look at the track. They're riding horses. I'll bet one will stay still for me if I can manage to stand on it."

"We should have never come here."

"Well, it's too late for that now. We have to try something."

Jessica kept her distance from the house because when she had come too close a motion detector turned some lights on and she had to dive behind bushes. It wasn't until then that she noticed the bushes were shaped like big dicks. Despite her situation it made her giggle.

She made her way around to the stables at the other end of the ranch and jumped over the horse fence. Her shoes landed in something gooey and a foul stink rose up all around her.

Damn it!

Scraping her shoes on the fence, she looked around for the large horse she'd spotted, but it was hard to see in the darkness. Figuring he may have wandered into the barn, she walked toward it and watched the ground, trying to avoid another landmine of manure. She was so focused on that, she didn't see the man emerge from behind the barn's door. He grabbed her arm before she even knew he was there. A small scream escaped her and she tried to resist, but his grip was strong. He had bulging muscles and a hard, unrelenting presence about him. She reeled back her foot to kick him in the balls but froze when she felt the gun poke just under her breast.

"Don't you dare, *perra*," he said.

He kept the gun in her back until they were inside.

Jessica wondered if Toby had seen them. If he had, he hadn't spoken up.

The gunman behind her looked even scarier in the light. His face was badly scarred and he was covered in intimidating tattoos of sombrero-wearing skulls, bloody daggers, and faded naked ladies. While most people had their barbwire tattoo around the bicep, this guy had it tattooed around his neck.

The room they entered was immaculate—far more gorgeous than any room in any house she'd ever been in. Art lined the walls next to framed posters for dirty movies.

"Sit down," the gunman said.

"Look, I'm really sorry, I wasn't trying to—"

"Sit down."

She did.

Trying not to look at him, she stared at her shorts and picked at the loose strings nervously. The gunman stayed there, standing, as if waiting for something. He had tucked the gun into the front of his pants, but that didn't make it, or him, any less frightening.

Once her breathing calmed, she was able to hear the noise coming from somewhere else in the house. It seemed to come from down the hall, reverberating in the dark corridor. It sounded like clapping. The sound wasn't steady. It held no timed pattern. There would be three real quick burst, then a pause, then two, then one, then a long pause and four more quick ones. Some would be loud and others would be mere whispers. Some sounded more like snapping, like a bungee cord being sprung loose.

Then the other sound came. It was moaning. It followed each clap, and when the claps got louder the moans turned into yelps. Then, as the snapping came in faster succession, the yelps turned to sudden bursts of screaming. As if motivated by the screams, the snapping and clapping grew louder, the pauses between them growing shorter and shorter.

Someone is being whipped.

She looked up at the man, but his face remained stoic. She wanted to say something, to ask something, but she couldn't find the nerve. All she could do was sit there and wait for whatever happened next, hoping it wouldn't be too awful. Jessica had no idea who these people really were. Toby said he recognized the woman, but he could have been mistaken, and even if she was a porn star that still didn't give Jessica a clear idea of her character. She was in a stranger's house, at gunpoint, listening to someone being whipped. Her situation didn't look good.

After a few more minutes of listening to the flogging, she heard a door open and high heels clacking. A young, black woman came walking out of the hall with a handsome man. His arm was around her shoulder and she was crying. They both wore white gowns. The man glanced at Jessica, but the woman was way too busy sobbing. Her face was drenched and her mascara had smeared all over her cheeks. They walked through the living room and made their way to the bar. With their backs to her, Jessica could see that their asses were bleeding through the gowns and the blood was running down their legs leaving wet, cherry red trails upon the hard wood.

More high heels clacked on the tile, and another woman came out of the hall. She was the one they'd seen at the lake—Kandi, Toby had called her—and she was wearing nothing but those heels and electrical tape covering her nipples. She was splattered with blood that didn't look like her own. Kandi saw her, turned to the gunman, and then looked back to Jessica.

"Oh, honey," Kandi said. "You've come to the wrong place."

The den was dark brown and very masculine, the kind you would see in liquor ads and cologne commercials. The man behind the desk was slim and much older than the others. He was smoking a cigar with his feet up. He smiled at Jessica as the gunman brought her to the chair.

"That'll be all, Javier," the older man said. "Please, see to the blood."

The gunman nodded and left without a word.

"So, sweet thing, what's your deal?"

Jessica tried to stay calm, but her limbs trembled.

"It's okay," he said. "You want a drink?"

The man lifted a remote control and pointed it at a towering cabinet. He hit a button and the bottom of the cabinet turned around, revealing a large assortment of shimmering bottles.

"You look like a lady who would prefer a chardonnay."

He got up and went to the stock. As much as Jessica wanted a drink to calm her nerves, the thought of date rape drugs flashed through her mind. She didn't want to take whichever one he grabbed first. She looked back to the desk and the half empty Bacardi bottle that sat there, the same one he'd been pouring himself drinks from.

"I'll take some of that rum," she said.

He didn't bat an eye.

"I aim to please," he said and grabbed a fresh tumbler.

He filled the glass, handed it to her, and sat back down. She slammed back half of it. She hadn't eaten dinner yet, so she hoped it would hit her fast and mellow her out. She was still hoping to talk her way out of the house and didn't want to panic and babble on in her fear. She wanted to come off strong and collected, a woman not to be fucked with, instead of some girlish victim.

"My name is Rutger Malone. Have you ever heard of me?"

"I don't think so."

"Well, I'm an old timer, and you're young. How old are you anyway?"

"Eighteen."

"Barely legal and oh so beautiful."

She shifted in her seat, crossing her legs protectively, and finished the drink in one more gulp. The burn made her eyes water and she pulled it in, not wanting this Rutger Malone to think she was crying.

"What's your name, girl?"

"Jess."

"Well, Jess. Would you mind telling me what you're doing here?"

She could have lied. She could have given him a fake name. But her fear had made her head hit a wall. Thinking the truth might be best anyhow, given that it was relatively innocent, she decided to go with it.

"I'm staying in one of those cabins across the lake. This afternoon my boyfriend and I saw that lady swimming. He said she was Kandi Hart, a porn queen. It got us excited. We just wanted to see what she was doing here. We thought maybe there was a porno being made and we wanted to see that."

"Is that all?"

She nodded.

"You weren't trying to steal my horses?"

"No. I got over the gate, but I was locked in. I was going to use a horse to climb back out."

Rutger chuckled at this. "Just a looky-loo, huh? Perhaps it's how sweet you look with all those freckles, but I believe you. You don't seem like a thief and you sure don't look like one."

Jessica looked at her shredded denim shorts and the pink wifebeater—and matching pink sneakers.

"You like porn?" he asked.

"What?"

"You heard me."

"Um, I guess I like it all right."

"Enough to want to see it being made?"

"Yes."

He got up and went over to her and leaned on the desk.

"I've been a porn film director for almost forty years," he said. "Guess how many dirty movies I've made."

"I don't know. Fifty?"

"Two hundred and thirty eight. More than five *per year*."

"Wow."

"I've done it all; straight, gay, threesomes, orgies. I've made cum-baths and fist-fuck features. I even made films that broke records. I shot Liberty Love having sex with eight hundred men in just eleven hours, a record before Lisa Sparkxxx banged a whopping nine hundred and nineteen men in just under twelve. I broke new ground, and so did Kandi."

Jessica didn't know what to say. Her mind was still reeling at the thought of fucking almost a thousand men in the time it takes for the sun to rise and fall.

"Kandi and I are making movies here," he said. "But from what you saw in the hallway, I'm sure you've gathered that what we're doing is more than just your basic stick and squirt."

"It's none of my business, Mr. Malone."

"But it could be."

There was a beat of silence between them filled only by the soft whir of the cabinet's cooler.

"What do you mean?" she asked.

"I'm asking you if you want a job."

Toby was crouched in the bushes, wondering what was taking Jessica so long. He hadn't even seen her come close to the fence yet and he felt like he'd been waiting there for at least half an hour. He wanted to call out to her but didn't want to alert someone inside or set off an alarm. As he'd told her before, places this ritzy often came with killer attack dogs or beefcake guards packing rods.

He left the bushes and came back to the gate. He looked at the house on the hill and saw shadows moving across the windows. The curtains were drawn but thin enough for him to make out the silhouettes of the people inside. There were at least four of them. On one of them, he could make out breasts with such definition that he knew the woman must be nude.

"Hey, Romeo," a voice whispered from the shadows.

Toby's spine locked and his heart seemed to stop beating. His air jumped back into his throat and he had to fight the urge to run. He wasn't even sure where the voice was coming from yet.

"Your little *puta* is inside," the man said as he emerged from the bushes. "Why don't you join us?"

The gate opened and the man waved him forward.

"Put your hands on your head, please."

Toby still hadn't moved. The man in front of him had a mean face and a no-funny-business body. His hands were like mallets made of spoiled meat.

"You a cop?" Toby asked.

"*Pendejo.* I am Javier. I worked for the man who lives here. I need to frisk you for weapons before you enter."

He didn't wait for Toby to comply; he just started patting him down and turning out his pockets.

"Where is she?" Toby asked.

"Inside, with her new friends."

Toby had trouble believing that and feared that their situation had gone from bad to terrible. He could still run, he thought. He wasn't on the grounds yet. The Mexican looked strong, but he didn't look fast, certainly not as fast as a teenage quarterback. But that would mean leaving Jessica behind. Anything could happen to her in the time it would take for the police to come all the way out to these sticks, and even when they did he and Jess could be brought up on trespassing charges, with intent to do whatever else.

"You're good," Javier said. "Come on."

He started walking up the path and Toby followed.

The four of them were sitting in the living room—Toby, Jessica, Kandi, and Rutger. It was decadent with high ceilings and droves of imported antiques. There was a glass coffee table between them and they each had a drink, except for Kandi. She had dressed and sat there, hands folded in her lap. She'd cleaned herself of the blood, but her makeup remained garish from the shoot, a glamour-ish whore look that excited Jessica.

"Bring us some *yayo*," Rutger said to Javier, and the Mexican went into a drawer behind the bar and came back out with the biggest bag of cocaine Jessica had ever seen. He plopped it on the table along with a straight razor with a bone handle.

Rutger cut out three slivers of coke and then pulled a green paper from his pocket. He stretched it out and Jessica saw that it was a hundred dollar bill. He rolled it tight, leaned down, and snorted up a generous line. Then he handed her the bill.

"That is yours to keep," he said. "Think of it as a down payment."

She rolled it tight, leaned down, and snorted up one of the other lines, all the while keeping eye contact with Rutger.

"You're a lucky man," Rutger told Toby while still keeping her gaze. "Not only is your girl dead sexy, but she also knows a good opportunity when she sees one."

Toby looked to Jessica for some kind of answer, but she was rubbing her nose from the coke. She had never snorted a line before. She'd only rubbed cocaine on her gums twice; first with Bruce and then another time clubbing with the girls. She loved coke and that was one of the reasons she tried to stay away from it; the potential for her to get hooked was clear and unwavering. She mostly stuck to ecstasy, other amphetamines (but never meth), and the occasional oxy. But she was in the palace of the big dogs now and the hesitation she'd felt earlier had bloomed into anticipation. The house reeked of riches and the people in it were wealthy, famous, and dreamlike to her. Even the Mexican thug was interesting, seeming like he'd just stepped out of a cult action movie. She was enticed by it all, and she wanted to partake in the splendor.

She tried to hand the bill to Toby, but he refused it. She

knew how he was. He didn't want to disappoint his parents or his precious team. So then she tried to hand it to Kandi, but she also turned it down, which surprised Jessica. She'd always had the idea that everyone in the adult film industry was a drug fiend. She would have offered it back to Rutger but he had produced a tiny spoon and was using it to do quick snorts. She slipped the bill into the front of her bra for safekeeping.

Rutger pointed at her.

"Don't you think she's beautiful?" he asked Kandi.

Kandi smiled politely and nodded. She seemed uncomfortable.

"By God," Rutger said. "We could have a new star on our hands."

A star? Me?

"What are you talking about?" Toby asked.

Shut the fuck up!

"I'm talking about movies," Rutger said. "Our movie in particular."

Jessica stirred in her seat. The coke was kicking in now and it made her even more excited about the prospects. She wasn't sure how Toby was going to feel about this, and she was glad he hadn't seen the two people with the bloody butts. He wouldn't have been able to handle that. But she could. She never minded playing rough. Bruce had introduced her to bondage. First he'd dominated her and then he flipped the game and she got to dominate him, a role reversal she surprisingly enjoyed.

"Now then," Rutger said. "You two wanted to get inside and catch a glimpse of what we're making, and frankly I am flattered. It's always nice to meet fans, especially when they're young, fit, and good looking, like you two.

"Thank you," Jessica said.

She could feel herself blushing like a schoolgirl. It was the man's power, money, and charisma that lured her in like a siren song.

"I'd like to offer both of you a job," Rutger said. "A couple of fresh faces are just what this picture needs."

Jessica saw Kandi tense even more than Toby did. She wondered if Rutger had angered her, she being the star. Jessica felt Toby's hand tighten on her knee and when she looked at him he was staring at Kandi like a dog at a food bowl. *Good*, she thought. *The hooks are sinking in.*

Rutger put a folder in front of her and opened it. There were pictures of three handsome guys inside.

"These are some of our studs," Rutger said. "At least one'll be in the picture, as well as Kandi, of course. What do you think of these men, Jessica?"

"They're pretty hot," she said, the cocaine making her talk faster. "They're smokin' hot."

Rutger turned to Toby and said, "I know you must be attracted to Kandi. You'd be a fag not to be."

Toby was still staring at her, but he seemed too star-struck to speak, so Jessica did his talking for him.

"She's his favorite porn star," she said. "He told me she was the first one he ever jacked it to."

"Jess!" His cheeks reddened.

"Calm down, I'm sure she hears that all the time, don't you, Kandi?"

Once again Kandi smiled politely, but her attention was on Rutger. She leaned into him and whispered something in his ear that made his smile falter.

"Excuse us for a moment," he said. "Help yourselves to the coke. Just take it slow now."

Rutger and Kandi stood up and walked toward the door to the den. He nodded to Javier and he came out from behind the bar with two bottles of beer and opened them before putting them on the table.

"Mr. Malone?" he said. "I need to make some deliveries."

"Just give us a few more minutes."

Javier didn't seem too happy, but he went back to the bar and stood behind it with his arms crossed like a sentry.

Once Rutger and Kandi went into the den Toby turned to Jessica, his eyes wide. He kept his voice low.

"What the fuck is going on here?" he asked. "Are they serious?"

"Of course, they are," she said. "Isn't this amazing?"

"It's freaking me out."

"What? Why?"

"He's got a star like Kandi, so what does he need us for?"

"He said he needed more people."

"But why not get more pros? Why a couple of nobodies?"

"Just don't blow this for me."

His eyes went even wider.

"What are you saying? You're actually going to do this? You can't be serious."

"I'm as serious as a heart attack."

"Well, I'm about to have one! I don't want you fucking other guys, especially not on film."

"You get to fuck your fantasy woman."

"You're okay with that? You'd want to share me?"

"I will be soon enough anyway. I mean, come on, Toby. You're going off to UT in a few months. Where do you think that leaves us?"

He looked away, resigning.

"You don't have to stay if you don't want to," she said. "Not back home or in this house."

"I don't think either of us should stay here. This place makes me nervous."

"Don't be such a baby. This is a big chance for me. You're already a somebody. You're going to play for the Volunteers, and maybe the Titans after that. But I really am a nobody. What am I supposed to do? Flip burgers? Fuck that. These people have money, Toby. They have fame. If they want to give me a slice of that pie, I'll do whatever they ask me to."

"Would you listen to yourself? You're willing to do anything they want?"

"Anything."

"What the hell are you doing?" Kandi asked.

"Don't worry," he said. "You're still the main attraction."

"We can't bring a couple of kids into this shit."

"Maybe not the boy, he seems skittish. But that Jessica is a ripe plum and I'm going to pluck her."

"These kids haven't even made regular porn yet, Rutger. They'll run out of here screaming if you put a cat-o-nine tails in their hands like you did to me earlier. You think either of them will rub one out while somebody gets their legs cut off?"

"Kandi, baby, you're getting ahead of things. Let me explain."

He sat down and motioned to her to do the same.

"You know those *Girls Gone Wild* tapes that made a killing?" he asked.

"Yes. They're crap."

"Total crap, but well marketed. They didn't even have any screwing in them, just regular girls getting naked. But, honey, that's what made them sell. People like to watch the process of a sweet, little girl-next-door turning into a sex-crazed, fuck demon."

"So you want some novices then?"

"Not alone, no. We're not just making titty tapes. What I envision is these kids being led into our world, on camera, by you."

"*What?*"

"You will be their guide, their concierge into the realms of pleasure and pain. Think of it: Kandi Hart, porn legend, taking two innocent newcomers and introducing them first to the craziest sex they've ever had, and then, slowly, step by step, to the darkest pits of human depravity. This is how we make a *good* film into a *great* film."

She let that sink in for a moment, seeing his point but still nervous about letting two teenagers they'd just met in on their filthy secrets.

"Can you promise me they won't get hurt?" she asked.

Kandi had the girl alone now, in the den. Rutger stayed with Toby in the living room, feeling that he was the one who needed more persuading. Rutger had asked her to woo him, but she insisted on talking to the girl alone instead. She told him it was the only way she would go along with this.

Jessica was indeed beautiful, and she was a natural redhead. She'd appeal to that niche market. She reminded Kandi of the ginger in *Mean Girls*, actually. She had a gorgeous face and dazzling eyes that failed to conceal the beast behind them. In many ways, she reminded Kandi of a younger version of herself. Maybe that was why she wanted to have a talk with her.

"I just want you to know what you're getting into," she said.

"I think I do."

"Really?"

"Hey, this guy wants to pay me to look beautiful, have sex with whatever hot guys I choose, and become a star in the process. All I have to say is *where do I sign*?"

"It's not as simple as that. Most girls never make it to real stardom. The Jenna Jamesons of this world are very few amongst the nameless many. Most girls last about two years in porn, and only seven if they go pro."

"Okay, but there's nothing to lose."

"There is, believe me. Once you do this, you can't undo it."

Kandi put her hands on the girl's shoulder.

"X is forever," she said.

Chapter Twelve

Much of Connie's body had been ruined by modifications. Her breasts, while huge, gave Harold no pleasure. Her once pretty face had become a collagen-filled mess and there were stitch marks behind her ears.

Christ, the things women will do to their bodies.

Most of her was unsalvageable, but there was one part of her that wouldn't be changed at all, and it happened to be what he most prized.

He was close up with the magnifying glass, inspecting her vagina for any imperfections. She was clean. She showed no signs of herpes or genital warts—surprising to him given that she'd screwed blacks, who he considered to be the most prominent carriers of all filth. No mites scurried through her bush and her vaginal lips hadn't taken on the dark, brown hue that made them look like meat left out too long. Her vagina was a fuchsia gem, like a blushing flower just opening in the warm light of spring. The clitoris was a pink pearl hooded by supple skin, and the opening was a perfect circle in the center of her welcoming sex. He wished he could still make it stretch from excitement. He always marveled at the muscle's ability to expand two hundred percent when fully aroused.

Carrie's was an excellent specimen and it held great sentimental value, just like Simone's tender hands. This was the first vagina that had taken him. It had flushed for him and accepted his manhood into its hot, moist tunnel. It was a wonderful vagina, very pretty and very special.

The scalpel was cold in his hand.

Vagina: Latin for the sheath, the holder of the sword.

He was just about to make the first incision when the doorbell rang. The sound carried all the way down to the basement. Maude was at home by now—their parents' old house, which they reluctantly shared—so he covered up Carrie and put the scalpel back on the track next to the scissors and scoop.

It's about time he got here. He said around nine and it's almost ten now. You'd think he was supposed to give me *money instead of the other way around.*

Harold came up in the elevator and opened the front door. The Mexican stood there glaring. It was just how the man's face rested. He always looked like he was about to strike, like a rattlesnake.

"Good evening, Javier."

He nodded once in reply.

"Well, come on in," Harold said, "before someone sees you."

Javier stepped inside and looked around. He always seemed very interested in the funeral room. One thing Harold liked about him was that the man showed no fear or discomfort around corpses. He didn't mind doing their business in the basement, which is where they went to now, just in case Maude forgot something and decided to come back. They rode down in the elevator and the silence between them was thick and pulverizing. Javier hadn't even spoken yet.

When they reached his sanctuary, Harold got the money from his safe and handed it to Javier, who counted it out slowly. Then he put it in his fanny pack and gave Harold the little grey bag of powder. Already Harold started itching, but he resisted the urge to scratch. He saw doing so in front of another person as an extremely low class act. But the itching was bad, almost as bad as when he would snort the heroin.

"This is primo China white," Javier said. "My cousin just moved in this shipment from Tijuana."

"Good, that dirt you sold me last time couldn't have been more than 40% pure."

"It takes longer to have an effect when you snort it like a *pendejo*. You should just shoot it up, then you wouldn't waste so much."

"I won't have my arms uglied by track marks."

"It's your money, *amigo*. Do what you want."

"Gee, thanks."

"By the way, the Marlins lost."

"Yes, I know. Tennessee needs its own team."

"You got the money?"

"Soon, really."

"You better." Javier jabbed him in the chest with his pointer finger. "A Benjamin isn't worth dying over."

Harold's chest was rattling. "Next week, I swear."

"Good. Need anything else? Coke? Maybe some underground porn? I even pimp now. I could get you some nice trim."

"No, thank you."

"Remember," Javier said. "Next week, or I'll come back."

Javier turned and saw Carrie lying there under the sheet. He pulled it off in a single thrust and stood admiring her. It was the first time Harold had seen him smile.

"Nice tits," he said.

The man is a barbarian.

First things first.

He wanted to complete the operation before blasting off.

He cut along the perineum and sunk the blade deeper around the skin surrounding Carrie's vagina. Once it separated, he scooped it away from the muscle tissue that connected it to her anus. He snipped the uterine veins and artery and tugged on the meat. Then he removed it from the lower part of her abdomen; first expunging the cervix, then the bulbous uterus, and then the delicate, white, almonds of her ovaries. It took time to carefully disconnect the entire vagina from the body, but Harold saw it as an artistic labor of love.

He placed it on a dish and admired it.

Even her fallopian tubes are lovely.

The euphoria of the dope hit him and he sat back in his chair and just stared at the ceiling. Oddly, there was a reddish hue when it normally had a puke-green shade to it, as if the mold he'd noticed earlier had spread. *But it looks more like dust than mold. Maybe something caused by the chemicals.* He wondered and his head tilted as he drifted into bliss. He'd done two quick snorts of the dope. He heeded Javier's word on its purity and decided to take it in baby steps, not wanting to risk an overdose. He was glad he did. The numbing buzz flooded his entire body, warming him like a bath after a long winter walk. His eyelids grew heavy and the itching commenced as it always did, but the numbing was taking care of that.

As the rush carried him into its delicious darkness, Harold thought about his pieces: Carrie's impeccable vagina, and Simone's beautiful face and arms. He had stopped thinking about why they had come to him this way, and now simply appreciated the gifts they'd given to him. But he did wonder who would come next and what treasures they would add to his collection. His drug-fueled mind conjured the image of an immaculate goddess, swimming in his now blood-red ceiling with the natural grace of a storybook mermaid. She had Simone's face as well as her hands, which ran down to the vagina, Carrie's vagina, and stroked the glistening bud of her clitoris. The goddess waved him toward her, curling Simone's bone-white finger.

I love you, she said. *We've always loved you.*

Chapter Thirteen

Jessica had messed around with girls before.

When she was on ecstasy she'd fool around with just about anyone, as long as they were good looking. She and the girls had fingered each other and licked one another's nipples, but she had never had another woman go down on her, the way Kandi did now.

Jessica was sprawled out on the bed in the schoolgirl outfit she'd been given. Kandi was in business attire—a white blouse, jewelry, glasses, a short skirt and high heels—and her hair was an amazing, blonde curtain. They were being filmed. They made out for a little while and then Kandi took off Jessica's panties and dove into her pussy with gusto. Kandi's tongue was now alive inside of her. She sucked the clit and lapped at her with great expertise, better than any man had ever performed cunnilingus on her. Jessica figured: *who better to know a woman's body than another woman.*

In the corner watching was Toby. He was supposed to start fucking Kandi, but he was too nervous and couldn't get it up. There was another girl kneeling in front of him and Jessica had been told that she was called a fluffer. They kept the stars hard or wet when they were off camera. She was doing her best with the blowjob, but Toby wasn't rising to the occasion. He'd never failed Jessica before and it was surprising to see him like this.

Jessica, however, was having a ball.

Kandi was gorgeous and Jessica had always appreciated a good-looking woman. She aroused her instantly and once they got into it, Jessica felt her hormones start to stir. Now Kandi was using her tongue and two fingers, and Jessica was positively sopping. Her toes curled and she clenched the sheet so hard that it sprung loose from one corner.

"Beautiful, ladies," Rutger said. "I'm sending in a present now. Be good to it."

Mia lowered the boom, and Ben moved in with the camera for a close-up on the door. It opened and in walked the tall, blonde stud, Billy Zap, the one she too had picked from the folder of pictures. They'd met only briefly before the shoot and she liked what she saw—the rippling abs, dimpled chin and country-boy smile. He wore a pair of tight jeans and already she could see that he could do what Toby currently couldn't. Billy came up behind Kandi and lifted her skirt, exposing her black panties and garter belt.

"I'm gonna make you quake," he told her.

"Bring it on," she said.

They spun Jessica through a fantastic threesome. Billy had a fat salami for a cock and he fucked Kandi while she ate Jessica's pussy until she came. Then Billy put it in Jessica's mouth, stretching it wide as he fucked her face, and soon he was pounding her pussy doggie-style while she took her turn and went down on Kandi. Jessica shuddered through her second orgasm and then cried out to Billy with her butt in the air.

"Fuck my ass!" she demanded, and he complied.

"You got it, baby," he said, his voice deep and low.

Her tight anus clenched around him for a while and when he pulled out, Kandi slid under her and adjusted Billy's cock so he could spray her face and Jessica's ass at the same time.

When it was over Jessica turned to the corner where Toby had been.

He was gone.

"You did good, baby," Rutger said, holding Jessica's head and kissing it. "You were fucking fantastic! Even I got a boner when you screamed at him to put it in your pooper."

She was still catching her breath. "Where's Toby?"

"I'm afraid he didn't work out as well as you did. That's okay though. Some people in this business really don't belong in the business. They're in porn for the wrong reasons and eventually they're compromised by personal conflicts with what they're doing. Better for him to bail out now than have regrets once it's too late."

"But, where did he go?"

"He just got up and left. I guess he went back to your cabin."

She was surprised, even a little hurt.

"Enough about him," Rutger said. "How do you feel?"

"Good. Great really. That was incredible. The sex was awesome but knowing that so many other people are going to get off on it made it *so much* hotter."

"That's what I wanted to hear! So you want to take this further?"

"Sure."

"What we just did was a warm up, to make sure you could handle it, and to make sure we could, you know, *trust you*. We're going to up the ante now."

"Ok. Just tell me when."

"Take a quick shower. We film again in half an hour."

Half an hour?

"Wear this," he said, handing her a dryer bag on a hanger.

Rutger walked back to the set to talk to his crew. Jessica unzipped the bag and looked at the garment inside.

Things were about to get much more interesting.

The skin-tight, vinyl policewoman's uniform was surprisingly comfortable, and Jessica loved the way her body looked poured into it. They'd gussied her up with rouge and heavy eye shadow and they had formed her hair into a flaming, moussed hurricane. She was a good foot taller in the leather boots, which matched her gloves, black aviators, and the baton that hung from her belt.

The room was empty, cold and silvery. She wondered if they'd be bringing a bed in or if she and whoever else would have to do it on the hard floor. She didn't know. She had no idea what she was about to do for this next shoot. The only direction Rutger had given her was to be strong and dominating. He told her to go with her instincts and to not hold back. She stood there waiting until he gave the cue, but even then she didn't know what to do, so she just put her hands on the wall, spread her legs and began grinding her ass in the air. She continued doing a little peep show, popping one boob out and then the other, but keeping the outfit on, knowing it had to be important.

There was a small door at the floor, like a pet door, and it came open and a chubby, hairy man came out on his hands and knees. He was naked except for latex paws on his hands and feet and a Halloween mask of a dog head. The mouth of it had been cut out and she could hear him panting.

Without getting into frame, Ben handed her a bowl of wet dog food. It stank in the way only wet dog food can. Jessica took it and looked down at the man who was wagging the fake tail that was attached to his ass by a rubber band. She saw what looked like some kind of pink powder puffing about him with every wag as she came closer to him with the food, and the man got up on his knees and pounced on her, slamming into her with his dusty hands.

She kneed him in the chest and he went *yipe*!

He waited patiently now.

"Good boy," she found herself saying.

She put the bowl down and the man began gobbling it up in a frenzy. Bits of food spattered across the floor as his ass wagged the tail harder and harder. She stood there watching the dog-man eat, waiting for more instruction from Rutger, but he offered nothing.

Once the dog-man had finished he began spinning in excitement and when she got close he rose up again and sprayed her with piss.

"Motherfucker!" she said, and she reared back and kicked him in the nuts.

He yelped again and fell onto his back. A slight plume of red dust rose from the floor in a mushroom and then vanished.

To Jessica's surprise, the man whispered "More."

She lifted one of her boots and saw him smile.

Then she came crashing down with the heel, crushing his testicles.

He howled and writhed and she found herself growing wet.

"Bad dog!" She reared back and kicked him right in his stupid, drooling grin, and when his hands went to his face she stomped on his testicles again. More dust swirled. Her adrenaline was pumping now and she felt a strange fury rising up out of nowhere; a rage from an unfair life and born of a newfound sense of incredible power and eroticism, and when he started barking she took the baton in her hand and started swinging, never wanting to stop.

Toby sat in the cabin watching dawn break.

Jessica still hadn't returned from the mansion. He

wondered what sort of insane sex she was having behind its white birch castle walls.

Seeing her have sex with Kandi had turned him on like nothing else, but he was so uncomfortable with all of those other people around that he couldn't get hard. This made him become self-criticizing and nervous, which only made matters worse. The fluffer had given him an oral treatment that any other time could have struck oil in mere seconds, but he was simply too stressed. Then, when that swinging dick, Billy Zap, had penetrated his girlfriend, he felt his heart drop into his stomach and he knew he couldn't stay there any longer.

Maybe Jessica had been right. Maybe they couldn't last in a long distance relationship. But facing that didn't mean his feelings for her just disappeared. He knew she was a wild child and that she'd very likely had more sex partners than he had, judging by her experienced technique and desires in the sack, but he never would have figured her for the type of girl who would spread her legs for people she had just met, and on camera no less. He'd learned a shocking truth about his girlfriend today and it disturbed him deeply. He felt as if he hadn't really known her.

He heard her walk up the porch and instead of coming in to greet him, or ask why he had left, or show any sense of consideration for him, she just tossed off her clothes and sank into the hot tub with the bubbles blasting. This sent him from morose to just plain mad. He got off the sofa and stormed out to the deck.

She looked dazed and he wondered just what other drugs that shyster director had pumped her full of. She didn't even seem to notice him. She just let the bubbles boil around her neck as she looked out at the strings of pink light silhouetting the tree line as it broke over the still waters of the lake.

"You can't even say hello?"

"Hello" she said, eventually.

"What is it? Are you pissed off that I left?"

"No."

"I couldn't stand seeing you like that."

"It's okay, Toby. I understand."

She still hadn't looked at him.

"Are you all right, Jess?"

"Yeah. It's just that I hurt my arm during a shoot, so Rutger gave me this *amazing* muscle relaxer."

"You know, you probably shouldn't take drugs from someone you barely know. How'd you hurt your arm anyway?"

"Swinging a baton."

"A baton? What the hell were you doing with a baton?"

A spark went off inside her eyes. "Having fun . . . having *lots* of fun."

"You sure seemed to enjoy letting that guy fuck you."

"He was pretty good."

"Oh, so I'm not?"

"No, of course you are. But he's a pro. Plus, I had Kandi. You really missed out. She's dynamite."

"Well, I'm glad I left. I never knew a porn shoot was so creepy. I wish we both had left."

"Well, I'm going back. I just needed some sleep first. They offered me a bed there, but I wanted to check on you."

"Yeah, right. All of a sudden you care."

"Don't be *that guy*."

"What guy? The one who doesn't like his girlfriend to star in porn? That's a pretty common guy, Jess. I'm not asking all that much."

"It's my body and my life. If you can't be happy for me than I have nothing more to say to you."

Her words cut into him like icicles falling from a roof—cold, vicious and totally unexpected. He thought about gathering his things and leaving her there. *Let her ruin her life in this filth.* He thought about breaking it off and cursing her name to everyone who would listen, including all the friends they shared. But the hurt was still fresh. There was still a part of him that thought it all could be repaired, that all they needed was to forgive each other, move past this mistake, and they'd be stitched back up, good as new.

Chapter Fourteen

Harold had sewn up Carrie's plump lips to give her a slight smile. It went over well with her relatives, including her parents who apparently were too grief-stricken to even recognize Harold. Not that he bothered to say hello. He kept to the shadows during the showings. He only wanted to savor in the mourners' pleased reactions to his work, nothing more.

He was surprised to see that Carrie had children. The elasticity of her vagina had held up remarkably well, considering. The fact that the kids were teenagers made him feel incredibly old.

When the wake ended, they all wrapped up and he had Glenn bring her back downstairs. Carrie was to be buried, and Harold still had some preparations to do. He was feeling sluggish today and was already thinking about the heroin, but he knew he didn't work well when under its spell and he had two more bodies coming in this afternoon. Maude was the funeral director and she got the details before he did.

"Two more stiffs after the wake," was all she told him.

Glenn finished up in the basement. Harold returned to it

and locked it up so that he could be alone with Carrie one last time. He'd made her look far prettier than any of those plastic surgeon butchers had. He'd shamed them with his finesse. He'd found out it was they who had killed her as well—a botched elective surgery. The quacks were paid millions to lose patients over nothing. It sickened him.

Knowing that she would be put into the ground in a few days saddened him too. He felt honored to know that he would be the last person to ever gaze upon her. She'd been a good girlfriend, up until the betrayal, which had ended them. She was funny, adventurous, and always horny. She taught him how to really make love to a woman; how to entice her, tease her and make her squirm. In exchange he had thrilled her with his knowledge of anatomy, performing cunnilingus on her with the individual parts of the vagina memorized and well understood. It was something she always begged him for.

He ran his hand through her hair and kissed her frigid forehead. The smell of the disinfectant had lingered under the perfume, and the bodies always got to be like blocks of ice after the embalming. But even in this arctic state of still life—or anti-life—she was Carrie, or at least what was left of her. Her hull still held her final dreams, fading memories, and lost desires.

"For old time's sake," he said, going to the cooler.

He hadn't wanted the freezer to frostbite the vagina before he could admire it some more. He placed it down on Carrie's giant breasts, right in front of her so she could see it. He stroked the public hair with his hand and leaned in to take a whiff. The cold of the fridge had taken some of its sweet pungency away, but it hadn't been distilled completely. He dove into her vagina, rolling his tongue upon the labia, just the way she liked it.

A thrum filled his ears and at first he thought it was more bass from a passing car. But this was one continuous noise. He looked around the basement. It wasn't one of his machines or the pipes overhead. He knew their noises well. But as he continued to look at the ceiling he saw the red dust he'd seen last night swarming above him in a spiraling motion. He'd attributed this to his high before, but now he was sober. The dust coiled, and the thrumming grew louder, as if it was coming off of the strange particles themselves.

A sound like rain rose up and he realized it was coming from Carrie's vagina. It grew louder, joining the bizarre thrum. Its labia parted and waved as air rushed out of the dead lips, and a moan of female pleasure escaped the vagina in a droning song, a swan song. The moan grew louder and Harold felt himself being drawn into it as if pulled in by hooks and chains. The moan was crying for him, aching for him, dying for him. He dove back into her vagina and lapped and sucked with fervor, romancing the cold vulva even more than he had when it had once pumped with hot blood and shuddering life.

Chapter Fifteen

"You should see what these guys have been making," Vic told him. "It will make you never eat again."

"In that case I'll pass," Rutger said.

"They made a tape where one girl spreads her pussy and another girl takes a dump right into it."

"I don't do disgusting, Vic. You know that. No feces, no vomit, and, as always, no animals."

"Well this shit sells, literally." Vic belched out a laugh on the other end of the call.

"Child pornography sells too, but I won't be a part of it."

"It's too bad. Those are a guaranteed hit."

"Trust me. We have a hit on our hands here. I have Kandi, and I have an eighteen-year-old porn-virgin costarring now. We get to see her progression. That's half the thrill."

"I don't know. It could take too long for her to progress into what we want to film."

"No way. She's *wild*, Vic. In one night I got her to crush a man's nuts and beat him half to death with a baton, and all he did was piss on her."

"That sounds hot. Send me the dailies."

"You know I never show incomplete work."

"But I'm the producer!"

"Trust me. This one will be worth the wait."

Kandi was getting a little worried about this set-up.

She and Jessica were wearing nothing but white butcher's aprons.

They were standing in front of the same metal slab Wally had sacrificed his arm upon. Lying across it were spiked mallets, kitchen knives, meat cleavers, hooks, and an old meat grinder with a turn handle.

She could tell that Jessica was scared too. Rutger had filled her nose with cocaine to get her amped, but now the energy had nowhere to go to except to fuel fear. Jessica put her hand in Kandi's and squeezed it hard. Kandi was glad to have it there.

Music started to play from the speaker overhead, breaking the silence between them. Music wasn't supposed to be added to the soundtrack until editing—along with sound effects made by yogurt and mud—but it seemed that Rutger wanted to set the mood. The music was a classic porn theme, complete with electric bass, strumming guitars, and cheesy synthesizer bars, like a cheap Curtis Mayfield rip-off.

"Breathe in the setting, ladies," Rutger told them. "Smell the metal. Feel the aprons on your skin. You are butchers. You live to carve meat. It makes you wet."

Kandi gave Jessica a wink, hoping to loosen her up.

"Action," Rutger said.

Jessica didn't hesitate. It was if she wanted the sex to calm her down by taking her mind to another place. She started kissing Kandi and their hands slithered up each other's curves. Kandi would have coaxed her up on the slab, but there were too many sharp things upon it, so she pushed her up against the wall, exposing the apple of her bottom.

Kandi began to spank her playfully and Jessica responded by shaking her ass and gasping with pleasure. They sucked, fingered, and scissored on the floor for a while, and just as they were finding a good rhythm with one another, the door opened and a man was shoved into the room with them. Kandi hadn't been briefed on another man to have sex with, and this wasn't Billy.

He was nude and had his hands cuffed behind his back. A leather gimp mask covered his face and the zipper was closed over his mouth. As he stumbled in, Javier followed behind him. Kandi looked at them, then at Rutger. He shook his head as if to say *don't worry about it*. She watched Javier lead the gimp up onto the slab. He then brought out a second pair of handcuffs and put them on the gimp's legs near his feet. He lowered a chain that was wound down from a wheel on the ceiling—Kandi had not even noticed it before—and attached a clip from it to the cuffs on the gimp's wrists. Then he left the room and closed the door.

Jessica got off the floor and Kandi followed her. As usual, they'd been given no instruction, but Jessica went to the man, spit in her hand, and then started playing with his cock. Kandi got up behind her and slid her hands under Jessica's apron to caress her tits. Kandi closed her eyes, allowing herself to be absorbed by the moment, and when she opened them again Jessica had a butcher knife in her hand and was gliding it across the man's erection. She wasn't cutting him, just gliding it back and forth upon the shaft as if shaving him, even though he was bare of pubes. There was an almost crazed look in the girl's eyes, and Kandi felt soiled watching the innocence leaving them. The eyes were fixed on the blade.

"Go for it, darling," Rutger told Jessica. "There are no taboos here."

The knife rose up to the man's nipple. Kandi noticed that there was a thin layer of powder on the blade, looking like the hyper-colored sand that was sold in tropical gift shops. She saw Jessica kiss the man's nipple and then she licked the blade clean.

"It's not too late to back out," Kandi whispered. "You don't have to do this."

"But I want to," Jessica said. "Oh, how I *want* to."

She sunk the tip of the blade right under the man's nipple and he flinched and pulled on the chain that held him. This made Jessica snicker. She curved the blade, encircling his nipple and slicing his flesh.

Kandi put her hand into the girl's crotch and slipped her fingers inside. She wasn't sure if she was trying to intensify the scene or just hoping to distract Jessica. Kandi was into S&M. She was turned on by the tapes she'd watched and she had to admit, at least to herself, that last night she orgasmed as she tore her costars' asses to shreds with the cat-o-nine-tails. Even when she witnessed Wally's amputation she managed to rub out a thunderous climax. But now a different mood had befallen them. There was an air of evil that filled the room, a carnal wickedness that had the crew foaming, and even Rutger looked tense with excitement. His body remained rigid, his eyes unblinking.

Jessica was dripping wet and her nipples seemed ready to pop beneath the thin cloth of the apron. She seemed cast away in the raging sea of her lust, and Kandi felt that there was no sanity here, no reason. There was only the vicious surge that comes with the absolute power over another human being.

Kandi watched as Jessica tore the nipple from his chest. It stuck to the tip of the knife and she flicked it to the floor. The man wiggled and moaned but put up no true struggle. His cock had actually grown bigger. She watched Jessica slash at him, and the blade danced in the air, glistening beneath the fluorescent light as it sent hot spurts of blood across the room. The stomach tore, the chest became slick, and the undersides of the arms opened like chicken cutlets. Blood covered the slab and the instruments in a sticky froth.

Wet red spilled across the floor. Dry, flaking red crawled the walls.

As if bored by the knife, Jessica threw it and the blade stuck into the wall. She picked up the mallet, looked at it, frowned, and tossed it aside.

By now, Kandi had also become aroused by the sadism. The smell of the blood got her loins in an unusual fury. It reminded her that she was truly alive. Kandi picked up one of the meat hooks and went behind the man. As she did so Jessica followed, knelt down behind Kandi, and started giving her a rimjob. Kandi took the meat hook and turned it upward. She let the point glide across the gimp's buttocks. It was sharp enough to cut him. She rolled the hook in the blood until it was nice and slick, and then sent it up into his asshole hard and deep.

The gimp squealed like an animal beneath his mask.

Kandi thrust the hook in and out, fucking him with it. Blood and liquid shit poured from his rectum and spattered on her hands and apron, but she kept on plunging it in. Jessica's tongue was all the way up her ass now, and Kandi ground back into her face for more.

The energy in the room was nearing frenzy. Kandi glanced around, and what she first assumed was blood on the walls now looked more like small bits of red matter, swirling through the air like sand in an updraft. She squinted, trying to see the red mist better, but her eyes were not what they used to be. All she could make out was a crimson cloud that drifted by, nebulous, so out of focus that she wondered if she wasn't just seeing things.

Jessica went back to the dangling gimp who was now drenched in his own blood. She began to lap at it, her tongue doing a hot samba on his wounds, burrowing it into them just as she'd done with Kandi's rectum. The blood smeared across her cheeks and splashed into her hair. She clawed at him and her nails dug in, mangling him. She seemed like a rabid cat, a human blender. She'd become a whore for gore. As she put the gimp's now flaccid dick in her mouth, she began to gnaw on it with her molars while scratching at his scrotum.

Something strange came over Kandi. She felt somehow alienated from herself, out of her own body. A dazzling red haze covered everything she could see, but it also covered her thoughts. In her mind's eye, visions of erotic horror thundered like the hammers of hell, all of them orchestrated by a thousand screams.

Kandi picked up the mallet, raised it high, and slammed it into the base of the gimp's spine. Jessica let out a bleat, spraying blood and spit in her fury, a ginger wolverine. Kandi slammed the man's toes next and Jessica got the gimp hard again. His inflamed cock pulsed with the percussion of his boiling blood.

Jessica slid the meat grinder down the slab and tightened it on the lip, her hands shaking. She took the gimp's scrotum and hard cock and pushed them down into the cup with one hand and began turning the gears with the other. Kandi watched in numbed shock as the gimp's genitals sank into the cup and twisted. Then the blood began to pool. Kandi gasped and the mallet fell from her hand. Jessica began screaming like a mad woman as she ground the gimp's manhood into a pulp that oozed out of the other side of the grinder. She bounced from foot to foot, delighted, a girl having just been asked out to her first dance.

Kandi backed away from the slab, her senses returned.

What am I doing?

She felt as if she had just awoken from a nightmare, and yet the horrifying vision still played on before her. It was as if she'd been drugged. She'd fallen into a sick trance and all she had wanted to do was rip the man to pieces. She enjoyed a little rough stuff, and if someone wanted their leg sawed off she wouldn't stand in the way of their depraved dream. But now she was part of a brutal slaughter. She didn't even know if the man would live.

What the fuck am I doing?

What the fuck is Jessica doing?

Unable to stand it any longer, she charged out the door

and threw the bloody apron to the floor. Naked, she marched down the hall without looking back. No one came after her. They were all too transfixed by the carnage. She came into the living room and walked up to the bar where Javier stood rubbing fingerprints from the glasses. He took one look at her approaching, put the glass down, and filled it to the brim with bourbon. Kandi took it, opened her throat, and tossed it back in one gulp. She slammed the glass onto the bar.

"Keep 'em comin'," she said.

"You were magnificent," Rutger said. "It was like seeing Elizabeth Bathory resurrected."

"I can't believe . . . I did that," Jessica said.

She had showered and was wearing one of Rutger's silk robes. Her hands were shaking and he could see that the nails were still stained red.

He started jotting in his notebook: *girl on girl in a bathtub of blood!*

"I don't know what came over me," she said. "I don't know if was the cocaine or what. I just . . . I wasn't myself in there."

She had a distressed look in her eyes. All the girls got this way in the beginning. It was natural. Rutger wondered if he had pushed her too far too fast. Even he hadn't expected the shoot to get as violent as the two ladies had made it. *Maybe I should tone it back*, he thought.

It wasn't like he didn't know the shock well. He'd been making these gory sex pictures for Vic for a few years now, and he had been desensitized, but filming some of these atrocities still left the acidic taste of bile in the back of his throat. He was no monster. He didn't get off on what he was making. He would give anything to go back to the glory days of making cinematic sex escapades, but that was yesterday. All he could do was accept his position and try his best to make beauty out of depravity. That's where he got off. He wasn't making some sex trade skin flick in a dirty motel room in Miami. He was making high quality, professional, semi-snuff. It had never been done before. He was, once again, a pioneer in his field.

"Don't worry," he said. "You did exactly what the producers wanted you to do. This was a slaughterhouse scene and frankly it was one of the best ones I've ever been a part of."

"But, that man . . . "

"You made his day, believe me."

"I turned his dick into hamburger!"

"He consented to this. Ederacinism is a big fetish in the underground."

"What is that?"

"It's where people get aroused by the thought of having their genitals ripped out by the roots. You just made a man's biggest fantasy come to fruition."

"I didn't know I had it in me to . . . to . . . *mutilate* someone like that."

"It's a lot to take in. But I'm paying three times what I paid you yesterday. You're doing so good, baby, don't let the newbie jitters get to you. You're going to be a huge star."

Her face whitened. "Will he die?"

"I doubt it. He's getting proper care."

Rutger was lying. The gimp was with the med student, but they lost performers to blood loss quite regularly. That wasn't his problem though. It's what Javier was there for.

"But what if he does die?"

"Jess, I can guarantee you that's not something you have to worry about. I run a strictly professional operation here. I know this is your first rodeo, but believe me I've earned my spurs."

She took a deep breath and ran her hand across her

forehead. She was sweating though the air conditioning was blasting, her flesh burned scarlet.

"You gonna be all right?" he asked.

"Yeah. I'm just in shock, I guess."

"Stay with us, Jess. This picture needs you."

"I'm not going anywhere. I just need to gather myself."

The scary part was that Jessica had liked it.

No, that wasn't true.

She loved it.

Jessica thought of the tearing, the sodomizing, and the grinding. She thought of the steaming meat of the man spattering across her chest and face in glistening chunks. It had thrilled her, and the memory made both her mouth and vagina water. The ferocity with which she had attacked him stunned her. She was impressed with herself. What she had told Rutger was true—she would have never expected herself to be capable of such violence. But the power she felt in that room, with another human being shackled to the butcher block, was better than any high she'd ever felt. It shamed cocaine and ecstasy, and it challenged great sex.

It made her want more.

It made her want to go *deeper*.

The only thing that still disturbed Jessica was her utter lack of control. It was as if she'd been possessed. She wanted to do what she was doing, and she enjoyed every moment of it, but there had been an unidentifiable force behind her actions, a frenzied energy that was frightening. Something had wafted up inside of her and had severed her conscious mind, leaving her walking in a pleasant nightmare. She felt no remorse in the thrall of this mood. There was no mercy in her heart and no satiation for her bloodthirst. There was only the strange red sand that had danced before her eyes, fueling her madness like the flap of a matador's cape before the eyes of a furious bull.

Chapter Sixteen

Toby searched online for more information about Malone but found no real dirt he could use to persuade Jessica away from the sleazebag. All he had found was a mile-long list of star-studded pornos the man had made over several decades. He doubted that Kandi Hart was anything other than a starlet in it for the cash, but he looked her up too, searching deeper than when he normally searched her. He found millions of hot pictures and videos but no dirt.

It was what Jess said about the baton that concerned him most.

The sex he'd seen her perform last night had been a basic threesome. It was nothing you wouldn't see in any standard skin flick. But the baton was a perversion he had trouble wrapping his mind around.

Was it being used as a dildo?

Cop uniforms were a basic dominatrix theme in porn, but Jess had mentioned the baton specifically, saying how she'd had fun with it. Somehow he doubted they would merely use it as a dildo. He had a feeling down in his gut that it had been used in the same way real cops used it. It was a vibe that he got from Malone's mansion. It was something in the way Javier had frisked him, something about Kandi's discomfort with having him and Jessica there. There was something dark going on in that place, he just wasn't sure what.

Toby thought about calling Jessica's mother, but he didn't know any number except Jessica's cell. He thought about the cops, wondering if he should call them. But the only thing he could give them was that there was cocaine in the place. It wasn't like Jessica had resisted them. She was no hostage. It was he who felt like a prisoner now. He was alone in the cabin, stuck there hoping that she wasn't doing what he thought she was. He couldn't bring himself to just leave her there, but he also couldn't bear to go back and see for himself what his girlfriend was really up to; at least, not yet.

Chapter Seventeen

The two bodies were mother and daughter.

They were in the same car when an eighteen-wheeler jackknifed and slammed into them, sending their car flipping into the grassy median that divided the highway. Both of them had been badly mutilated, especially the mother, who had been in the passenger seat.

The girl was only sixteen.

Her mother had been giving her driving lessons.

The mother's face had been annihilated by the side window, which had imploded upon impact. A chunk of twisted metal had nearly decapitated her, but instead had taken her right arm off at the elbow. Her chubby torso was a blob of blood and broken glass.

Most of the girl's damage had been internal. The air bag failed to deploy and the steering wheel hit her chest with such force that her ribs had splintered inward and punctured her lungs. Her neck was broken and her face had been ripped apart by the shattered glass, but the rest of her body was as pristine as if she had just been born.

Harold marveled at her sweet, virgin flesh; so pale, so

new. Pink polish was on her fingernails and toes. Her hair was naturally blonde and hung all the way down to the small of her back. He used it to cover her bruised, bashful breasts, making her look like a young Lady Godiva. Looking into her eyes he saw that they were green. It was a rare trait, and admirable, but he was holding out for brown; a gentle, earth-toned shade just like Tiffany's. Still, the hair was worthy of scalping and the feet were keepers.

He'd always despised the feet of grown women. They didn't match the rest of their bodies. They were calloused and had thick veins running through them. Once they reached a certain age they became blemished with varicose veins as well. Worst of all, they were almost always too big. Harold found this to be grotesquely masculine.

But a sixteen-year-old girl had perfect feet. They were small, pink, and puffy. He imagined himself playing *this little piggy* with the little buds of her toes. He lifted one of her feet and tongued between the gaps, letting his saliva wake up her skin to release their fragrance.

He didn't care what the mother was named.

He lifted the tag from the girl's perfect toe.

Amy.

Then he saw the last name on the tag.

Knowles.

Of course, he thought.

Harold had never been in any kind of relationship with Margo. He had simply stolen her panties.

When he and Carrie had shared an apartment, there was a seedy laundry room on the bottom floor of the building where the tenants could wash their clothes and buy sodas, chips, and condoms from vending machines. Harold and his girlfriend shared the chore, taking turns each Sunday.

They had already being living there for a year by the time he first saw Margo. He was sitting on the bench reading a magazine he had no interest in while he waited for his load to finish. He looked up at the sound of the door's ringing bell and saw a voluptuous brunette come in with a plastic hamper braced on her cocked hip. It was a hot day in August and all she wore were tight shorts, flip-flops, and a lime green halter-top. The top seemed ready to burst from the sheer girth of her chest.

Harold had always been very attracted to Carrie. She was a good-looking woman and electric in bed. But she did not have the generous, bombshell body that this woman did. It was as if she had stepped out of a pinup calendar from yesteryear or a Russ Meyer movie. Her eyes held his gaze when she caught him staring, and even though he was busted he keep right on doing it. She seemed amused by this and took to teasing him, putting down her basket to buy a soda, then rubbing the can across her cheeks and arms to wet her body. She twirled her hair with one finger and took long swallows of the drink. When she finally got to the laundry, she bent over at the waist and made a show of separating each one of her panties and bras before dropping them into the machine.

Then she walked out and waved to Harold without even looking at him.

Before the machine could ruin them by getting them clean, Harold reached in and grabbed a handful of panties and two bras. Alone in the laundry room he brought the bundle to his face and inhaled deeply, savoring his prize.

During the months that he, Carrie, and Margo all lived in the apartment complex, Harold saw Margo on several other occasions. The first time following the underwear incident was just a passing in the hall. When he saw her approaching the mailboxes, a jolt of guilt-induced horror ripped through him like a bolt of lightning. He tried to gather his letters and duck away, but she had come up too fast. She spotted him and gave him a knowing wink, and all he was able to do was trot away toward the stairs with his head hung low. But he had seen her name on the mailbox.

Margo Knowles.

Margo knew he had taken her underwear. She had to know. But she didn't call him out on it. Maybe she thought it was funny. He wondered if perhaps it was even a turn on. He was too chicken-shit to make a move though, not so much because he was faithful to Carrie, but because he could never imagine that a buxom sex-kitten like Margo would ever be interested in his skeletal body and nervous, black eyes. Margo was the type of girl who would run with the cliché bodybuilder guys with their fast cars, footballs, and forearms; the very same guys who had smacked his books from his hands in high school and tried to pull his boxer shorts up over his head while he was still in them. She may have smiled at him, but if he made a move that smile would turn to the cruel laughter that only a pretty girl can produce.

He saw her sporadically—swimming in the pool in her too-small bikini, pulling in and out of the parking lot in her convertible, and even shopping at the grocery store down the street. But he never saw her in the laundry room again; no matter how much he varied the days he went. Eventually she moved away, and Harold never saw her at all. He was left with just those few, precious memories of her, and the secret shoebox of shame that he kept hidden from his girlfriend.

Over the years, the memory of Margo and her perfect body had faded into the background of his erotic daydreams, and the contents of the shoebox also became less and less alluring until one day he had discarded them all together.

He wished now that he had kept at least one pair of panties, just so he could compare them to the ones she wore now, which, if they were any bigger, could pass as a beach towel. It wasn't just the mutilation that had made her unrecognizable; it was the undulating rolls of blubber that she'd packed on over the last twenty years. Had it not been for the photographs of her that the family had provided, he would have thought it was a different Margo Knowles all together.

But that wouldn't make sense now would it?

No.

There was a method to this, Harold knew. One after another they were coming to him—returning to him—these women from his past. The dark hand of fate was bringing them to him so that he and he alone could snip, cut, and tuck their bodies, and preserve what had made them so beautiful to him.

It was *in the flesh*.

Even Amy, Margo's daughter, belonged to this growing train of his own personal admiration for the female form. She was the daughter of a woman he had long lusted after—flesh of her flesh, blood of her blood. She had sprung from her womb in a warm gush of blood, back when Margo still possessed the beauty that had driven him mad enough to steal panties. This girl had soaked up Margo's beauty like a sponge and was only beginning to show it as she blossomed into womanhood, only to be struck down by the annihilating backhand of a hungry reaper.

Simone and Carrie had their parts that he had selected as choice cuts.

But Margo's prime selection was not a cut from her own body—it was from what her body had produced.

Chapter Eighteen

"*I don't think* I can keep doing this," Kandi said.

But she wanted to.

She didn't want to abandon all that money, power, and art.

But she had to—didn't she?

"Don't bail on me completely," he said. "Perhaps we can make some changes."

Rutger was sitting next to her on the curved, outdoor sectional set. His morning Bloody Mary sat on the fire pit's lid. In the pool, Jessica was splashing beneath the fountain, naked and as carefree as a child, which Kandi herself had been back when she was at the peak of her stardom.

"I don't know," she said, looking away.

"We could change the level of your involvement."

She felt a twinge inside of her. "How so?"

"Simple. Jessica is really shining. We could shift the focus to her and put you more in the background."

The water glistened in the sunshine and so did Jessica.

"I don't play second banana to anyone," Kandi said.

"That would be my preference."

"I just feel like my nerves are frying out."

"That's the price we pay. Art comes from pain."

He took a long sip of his drink and then put his hand over hers.

"You need to trust me," he said. "These feelings you're having, the fear and disgust, they'll fade over time."

Those feelings, powerful though they may be, paled in comparison to the bloodlust she'd felt. The fury that had overcome her was terrifying. It was so alien, as if she had fallen into some sort of ultraviolent fugue state. She had become an animal. So had Jessica.

"Without fear and disgust to hold us back, don't we risk going out of control?" Kandi asked.

"I certainly hope so," he said with a laugh. "Otherwise we don't have a film."

The glass door behind them opened and Javier came out. "Would you like breakfast now?"

Rutger looked at Kandi and she shook her head.

"I think we're all right for the moment," Rutger told him.

He turned to go back into the house, but Kandi stopped him.

"I'll have one of those Bloody Marys, please."

He nodded and walked off, and as he did, Rutger turned to her and patted her hand once more.

"That's the Kandi I remember."

Jessica hadn't come back to the cabin last night.

Toby had waited up for her like a fool and passed out in the chair. Now the morning sun pierced his eyes like rusty nails. Feeling the empty bottle of bourbon in his lap, he knew why the light, and his sudden movement, brought so much pain. The throbbing in his skull reminded him of when he'd received a mild concussion on the field last year. The whisky's poison kicked his brain around like a hacky sack and made his bowels churn.

Toby stood up slowly and let the bottle tumble to the floor. He squinted in the light and looked across the lake to the mansion. A sickening thunder boomed in his guts.

He wanted to hurt Jessica the way she'd hurt him. He wished he could break up with her, break her heart, but she'd already dumped him. She hadn't given him the speech, but she didn't have to—her actions said it all. A big part of him told him to just leave the cabin early and let her new friends take her home, if she would ever leave them at all. But there was a bigger part of him that wouldn't be able to handle the nag of curiosity and, though he hated to admit it to himself, the worry.

He started to wonder if this was his fault. Maybe the fact that they had never really talked about what they would do when he went off to college, a five-hour drive from their hometown of Humboldt. He had given consideration to them moving in together, but they were only eighteen. It seemed too big of a move. In addition to this, he was a little scared of her. She was so sexually aggressive and she craved danger of all kinds. There was a wickedness to her that was both sexy and frightening. He cared for her, maybe even loved her in a way, but she was too unstable and it made him retreat from thoughts of commitment.

Jessica was right. They weren't meant to last. But he hated to see it end this way, and more importantly he would never forgive himself if something bad happened to her, which he felt was highly possible.

Nauseous and depressed he shuffled to the bathroom.

He wasn't sure which end to put to the bowl first.

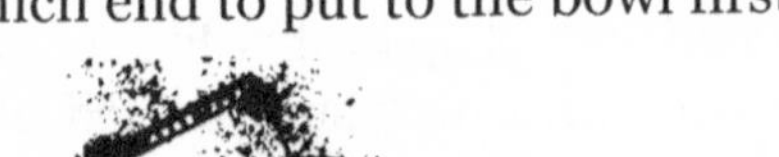

"We need to go further with the next shoot," Rutger said. "What do you have for me?"

Javier opened the briefcase, removed a manila folder, and handed it to him across the desk. Rutger sifted through them while petting Cougar, the cat purring like an idle motorcycle. She would need a grooming soon. Her fur was caked with red sand. He didn't know what she had gotten herself into.

There were not a lot of lookers in the folder, except for a young, beautiful black girl. In the picture she looked highly distressed. Tears filled her eyes. Her body was full and tender.

"Tell me about this one," he said.

"Tynice Porter. Seventeen-years-old. She is the daughter of Jackson Porter, the industrialist. He moved into Vic's market and was stealing our customers, so he had us abduct her and we held her for ransom."

"Porter won't pay it?" Rutger asked, surprised.

"No, he paid it. But Vic didn't give her back. She's in a warehouse."

"Jesus. Well, what will she do?"

"Anything we tell her too. She just wants to live."

"She a virgin?"

"If she was, she isn't now. Not after what we've done to her. We had to send pictures to Porter to motivate him to pay. He was trying to bargain with Vic."

"I don't think I want to do a rape shoot."

"They sell."

"Pass."

"She's a good piece of ass, believe me."

"Pass."

Rutger took a closer look at some of the men and women in the dossier. He felt like they'd been beating up and grinding a lot of men. It was time to bring another lady into the mix. He found a decent looking one who would look much better in full makeup.

"What about this one?" he asked.

"She's a willing participant, another mental case with a fetish. She gets off by hurting animals."

"Unless we're gonna shoot her in her bitch face, I'm not interested. I don't allow that. Pass."

The final woman had a sour face but full, natural breasts that were at least D-cups.

"How about this one with the udders?"

"That's Sandy. She's done some cheap stuff for us before, mostly tit bondage. She loves painkillers so that's what she gets paid in. She had a baby recently and those tits of hers are lactating. *Caliente. Caliente como el infierno."*

"A little too common of a fetish. Will she do anything more? Have her tits cut up maybe?"

"No. Those *tetas* are her money makers."

"These men all look like the same old boners. Just a bunch of lowlifes willing to take a beating for some pussy."

He tossed the folder on the desk and leaned in to Javier.

"I need something extreme," he said.

"Then take Tynice. Kill her if you want."

"I couldn't live with that."

"She's gonna die either way."

"Well, not here. Besides, the girls aren't ready to go that far. I want their progression to be in steps. They're coming along well. The film is tight."

"You're the director."

"I want something with hardcore shock value. Dead to rights."

Javier paused, rubbing his chin. "Dead?"

"Yeah."

Javier leaned back and made a temple with his fingers. A rare grin spread across his face.

"I know a guy," he said.

Chapter Nineteen

His collection was thriving: Simone's face and arms, Carrie's vulva, Amy's feet and legs. Harold admired them while the last of the dope took effect, and he dreamed of more lovely plasma, corpuscles, and sinew. His mind reeled with images of tearing muscle and supple dead bodies.

A buzzing like hornets filled his ears.

An image of Laura Shaw flooded his consciousness.

Harold's memories of her naked body grinding beneath his flashed and bloomed. He saw her breasts heaving and sweat collecting at her naval in a tiny, shimmering pool. Her stomach was pale silk, white jade. Her torso came upward in a small V, ending with the spout of a swan neck and a perfectly-structured skull—the high cheekbones, the heart-shaped jawline and the straight teeth with no gaps.

She'd been one of the last girls he dated and the one who had introduced him to heroin. She was a functioning junkie then, unlike what she later became. Last he'd heard she was in rehab for the second time. But when he was with her she was full of life, particularly the nightlife. She lived for the rush of her Harley, loud clubs, the spike of cocaine at midnight, and the drift of heroin at nine in the morning. She was a beautiful mess, a woman without self-control or inhibitions, with a strong body and a restless heart, and Harold fell for her like an anvil thrown from a tall building. He had a hard crush and wanted them to be exclusive, but it was a desire she did not share. Laura wanted freedom and that included all the men and women she cared to bed, if they made it to a bed at all. Harold was one of those lucky lovers, but he would never be the one and only.

All signs pointed to her being next.

This is the way it is supposed to be, he thought.

Looking past the collection, he saw Amy's reconstructed corpse lying there. He'd done an impeccable job on the girl. He put more stitches in her than the Bride of Frankenstein, but the mangled remains had come together with the right putty and plaster. He filled in her cuts and powdered them over, casting a pallor veil over the flesh. The casket would cover her lower body. No one would notice the absence of her legs.

As he went into a nod, he looked at her face with pride, noting that he still had to sew her lips shut before the service. As if her body was somehow awakened by this thought, her mouth opened, just slightly at first, but then wider, so wide that it seemed she might dislocate her jaw.

This sight snapped his eyes open with disbelief. He was having these visions more and more now, even when he was sober. But they were more than mere visions. They were tangible, touchable, breathable, and the red dust that brought them was everywhere. He swept and swept, but it piled up in corners and stained the ceiling and the walls. Something was germinating in his sanctuary and it seemed to guide him in both body and spirit.

He watched Amy's mouth contort as a swarm of strange bugs emerged. The insects spun in the air in a cyclonic pattern and their buzzing echoed in the crypt, a cacophony of insectile static. He watched them crawl across the ceiling.

Then their bodies went from black to sudden neon red. Their light throbbed in them like they were fireflies only larger, and their light not only flickered, it made circles in the air that grew and stretched like a moving lens flare captured in an old movie. Their movements became dancelike and the hum of their white noise was oddly musical. He found himself standing on wobbly legs, reaching up to the swarm, and welcoming them as they flew down to his body and mummified him in a crimson shroud.

Laura came to him that night.

The moment Glenn brought the body in, Harold knew it was her. He didn't even need to look under the sheet. He could taste her in the air, a faint fragrance of lilies and dead cells. Glenn turned to leave. In the dim light, he clearly hadn't noticed the hint of red that Harold could feel scattering like tiny lightning in his own pupils.

Harold brought the gurney under the lights and prepared himself for the big reveal.

Laura Shaw was even more beautiful than he remembered. The years had been very good to her. It was clear that she worked out often. Taut abs without looking too butch. Arms that didn't jiggle, and no signs of cellulite on her legs. Her breasts were high and firm and that perfect bone structure of her youth had not been compromised over time.

"Oh, my darling," he said, running his hands all over her.

Turning her arm over he saw the track marks. There were not enough of them to make her a junky. She was a party girl, same as always. The heroin had not broken down her body; she'd just taken one shot that she couldn't handle, and now she was his, all his.

He leaned over and kissed her lips and ran his tongue over her perfect teeth. His chest heaved and he felt the insects rising up. They flew inside of his lungs and up into his throat. He could feel the warmth of their glow as they exited his body and poured into Laura's in a squall of crimson light. With his hand on her stomach he felt it swell and the coldness of death began to ebb. He felt her flesh become warm again as if she was alive.

A gift.

He removed his clothes in a hurry and then climbed onto the gurney. He spit into his hand and gave his already hard cock a few strokes. When he touched her vagina, he found that it was already wet, the clitoris swollen to the size of a cherry tomato. He moved in and her vaginal walls closed around him tighter than they ever had when she was alive.

The red dust filled the air like a storm.

Part Two

Goddess

Chapter Twenty

Shattering bone.
Jetting blood.
Hard cock and flushed pussy.

Jessica punched the woman in the face again, and this time the brass knuckles shattered her cheekbone and sent teeth out of her mouth and onto the floor. The woman had agreed to a beating, but Jessica had taken it much further than that. She was holding the woman's hair in a ponytail and the woman had stopped moving her head all together. While she was unconscious, Billy still didn't stop fucking her.

Jessica didn't know much about health or anatomy, but she did know that if the woman stayed blacked out for more than a few minutes, she could have permanent brain damage, and if there was internal bleeding, she could die.

Jessica didn't care. In fact, it turned her on all the more.

She spun around and climbed on top of the woman, presenting her ass and vagina to Billy. He took her offer and began fucking her deep, to the hilt, as if he was trying to bust through Jessica's cunt and into her guts. She found herself screaming as her eyes rolled back and her toes curled. A blissful dizziness overcame her. She wasn't sure if it was the high of the violence, the sex, or the pills the two of them were given an hour before the shoot. Either way, they were buzzing hard and Billy was slamming her like a battering ram.

In the loveseat across from them, Kandi sat in a drunken stupor. She was fingering herself beneath a Little Bo Peep costume, but Jessica could see that her heart wasn't in it. A group of four men, extras brought in for just this scene, were having a circle jerk around her, each taking their turn cumming on her face. Their own faces were hidden behind sheep masks. When they ejaculated, they bleated and brayed like lambs.

Billy was still fucking Jessica when Rutger told everyone to cut.

Consternation furrowed his brow and he put his hand over his eyes. Mia lowered the boom and turned away from the scene. Ben looked to Tye, who had been sweating, his dark face pinched and sour. Lately he and Mia had been vocal about getting increasingly hesitant to film these brutal scenes.

Billy began to pull out, but Jessica moved back onto him, silently demanding more. And she was pleased to feel him keep thrusting into her like a jackhammer. Her body quaked, just as he'd said that it would.

"This isn't working," Rutger said. "It was good before this one passed out. Good job fucking on top of her. But something has gone stale. I can't put my finger on what's wrong, but I'm bored and the audience will be bored too."

Jessica could barely process his words. She was ready to cum.

"Kandi!" Rutger called. But Kandi was slumped over, dripping with semen. Unresponsive. "Christ, she's *shitfaced.*" He paced back and forth. "And where is this fucking dust coming from? We need to get the maid out here more often."

But Jessica and Billy didn't care about the floor. Billy dug his nails into her back harder. They scratched her like gentle razors and the hint of pain delighted her. She moaned with each scratch and thrust.

"Come on, baby," she said. "*Hurt me!*"

Billy dug deeper and his nails sliced her. But Jessica wanted more, much more. She kept thrusting backward into Billy, smashing into his pelvis, screaming.

"Roll camera!" Rutger pointed at the crew.

Jessica looked over, seeing a glimmer of revelation in Rutger's eye.

"Billy," Rutger said, "don't you dare cum yet." He turned to Javier. "Get your tool box."

Javier exited the room in a hurry, moving around Mia who was struggling with the boom, her hands shaky, her face pale as ivory. Jessica savored the look of nausea in the woman's grimace.

"Hit her," Rutger said.

Billy smacked her ass and Jessica groaned.

"Hit her in *the face!*"

Jessica turned around to look at him, smiling, asking for it, and she received it.

They kept going like that, Billy pounding her with his cock and slapping all of her cheeks. She roared and frothed like a mad dog. Billy changed course and slammed his erection into her ass. He used no finesse, just slammed it up in there as quick as he could. The pain and the pleasure became one inside of Jessica, churning like fire and then igniting and spreading through every inch of her body.

"Don't you cum," Rutger said.

"Don't you dare," Jessica added.

"Not yet, baby," Billy said. "You need more punishment!"

He changed his rhythm to hold back. Jessica knew it couldn't be easy for him. He was pulsating inside her, ready to burst. She admired his perseverance and awaited his promise of further pain.

Javier came back into the room with a rusty toolbox and popped it open. Rutger sifted through it and then tossed Billy the garden hoe. Seeing it, Jessica felt the wheels of another orgasm spinning in her womb.

Come on, you fucker, hurt me!

Billy picked up the hoe and scratched her back with it. He cut a little deeper with each raking and soon she could feel the blood all wet and sticky. It spilled into the crack of her ass and rode her ribs and beaded at her nipples. She grabbed the woman's head and began smashing it into the floor. Jessica started to yell in beguiled pleasure. The ruckus stirred Kandi and she got down on the floor and crawled over to Jessica. Positioned face to face, Kandi's still slick with semen and stained with mascara tears, they kissed, and then Kandi moved to Jessica's back and started lapping at her gushing cuts.

"So what about this guy you know?" Rutger asked, looking out at the setting sun.

"I'm seeing him tonight," Javier said.

"What's this special thing he has to offer?"

"I thought you hated ruining surprises."

The sky had fallen to a blazing red that reminded Rutger of all the blood he'd seen today. The maid would have her hands full getting it out of the tile.

Javier took a long pull on his blunt and offered it to Rutger.

"No thanks," he said. "It makes me paranoid."

"I'll be back in a few hours," Javier said. "You'll be pleased."

Now the red in the west reminded Rutger of the dust that had been collecting in his house.

"Have you noticed all that sand?"

"Yes."

"I guess it's coming from the lake. I don't know who keeps tracking it in. I'm letting everyone know to be sure and wipe your feet. This place gets messy enough without dirt."

"It's not the lake."

"What?"

"It's not the lake. It's in the warehouses too. We can't get it out."

Kandi took a long, cold shower in an effort to sober up. It helped, but it wasn't a surefire cure. The booze ravaged her just like it had in the old days and her mind was even more sore than her vagina. She tried to wash the memory of Jessica's blood from her thoughts as well as her mouth.

Kandi had experienced a lot of bodily fluids in her mouth over the years, but this was new territory. She wanted to blame the alcohol, but she couldn't. It had never hit her that way. She knew that it was the unexplainable bloodlust again. It had seized her in its sinister vice grip, overpowering her with its mad rush, refusing to yield and growing more potent when she had thoughts of resistance. It frightened, but also pleasured. It was more than adrenaline, more than sheer sadistic delight. There was a rush to it that was otherworldly now. It filled not just the body, but also the spirit itself. She was chained by its command and yet she felt unchained from her own moral restrictions, from reality itself, and this was a form of bliss she had never imagined possible this side of heaven. It was something she'd never been able to buy with money and had never felt in the throes of all the sex she'd ever had. Even the joy and acceptance she'd felt in David's loving arms could not compare to the bloodlust. As much as the aftermath sickened and terrified her, the ride getting there was undeniably euphoric.

Toby awoke in the dark.

The hair-of-the-dog beers he drank had relieved his headache, but it also lulled him into much needed sleep. He stayed up too late last night waiting on Jessica, watching Rutger Malone movies on his phone in the hopes of getting deeper into the man's mind.

He got off the couch and went to the deck. The night air was fresh and he listened to the trees rustle. There was an ambience to the world that seemed unfair given how he felt. The sad jealousy he had felt over Jessica had now soured into silent anger. He was angry with her, but he was downright furious with Rutger Malone for ensnaring Jessica in his filthy underworld.

She had been gone for over twenty-four hours now. He thought again about the police. If he got them to visit Rutger's place maybe he could at least find out if Jessica was all right. No matter how enchanted she had become by her new profession, he still had trouble understanding how or why she would leave him alone in the cabin for so long. She must know how he would worry and how crushed he would feel. He had a hard time believing she could be that cold.

"I can't take this anymore," he said through gritted teeth.

He went back inside to get his sneakers.

Chapter Twenty-One

The doorbell surprised Harold and he stopped cutting.

He went to the intercom.

"Who's there?"

"Javier."

It hasn't been a week yet. Christ, I need more time, you greedy spic.

"I'll be right up," Harold said.

He knew better than to anger the man.

He let Javier in and they went down to the basement together. Harold had not bothered to cover Laura and her limbs sat in a neat pile beside her torso. She wasn't having an open casket service, so he'd be able to dive into her with gusto. He was just about to remove her face and he hoped Javier would not keep him from his art long.

"I have a proposition," Javier said. "My employer is willing to erase your debt and buy you half an ounce, unless you'd prefer cash, or a spin with one of our girls. I still think you could use a good lay."

Not anymore.

"In exchange," Javier said. "You will give us access to the bodies."

Harold felt his blood drop a few degrees.

"You can't be serious," Harold said. "I can't take that risk. It could ruin the business."

"I am serious."

"The answer is no."

"You're in our debt."

"And I will pay you." Harold felt the veins pulsing in his neck.

"But this is the cost."

"What? I owe money not—"

"The price has changed."

"You can't do that!"

Javier frowned and showed his teeth.

Yes, he can.

"Refusal will be considered an insult," Javier said. "You don't want to insult me or my employer."

"What do you need dead bodies for?"

"The same thing *you* need them for, right, Dirty Harry?"

Javier reached for Laura's torso and twirled his finger in her pubic hair. It made Harold fume and he struggled not to show it.

"You want to fuck them?"

"Not me. You think I'm sick? For movies."

"Jesus, you want to film it too? What if a member of the family happens to get a hold of one of these little movies?"

"Don't be a pussy. Think about what you gain."

Harold sat upon his stool in sour defeat. There was no argument that would get him out of this. Javier was a man who got his way. The people he worked for were as mysterious as smoke and, Harold knew, were as deadly as the snakes that shared their cold blood.

"Just don't film it here," he said. "Please."

"You have a hearse, right?"

"Right."

"Arrangements can be made."

Javier looked down at Laura's torso.

"For now this one comes with me," he said.

Ruins.

His masterpiece was broken, as was his heart.

Harold remained in the stool while Javier let himself out with Laura's torso wrapped in a garbage bag. Sitting there, Harold looked at the arms and legs, wishing he'd had time to decapitate her.

I should have hidden the body, he thought. *She's so precious.*

Why did I leave her exposed for that bastard?

He took Laura's right hand and interlocked their fingers. She held him tight, expressing affection.

It's not your fault, she said.

Her other arm slithered toward him and its hand caressed.

They were such lovely arms and the legs were equally beautiful. He realized he had been foolish. There was no need to collect just one of each thing. Beauty was beauty. All could, and should, be preserved. He took the arms and legs over to the collection on the table. Simone's face smiled up at him and Carrie's vagina turned scarlet.

Love, they both said, and Laura's hands reached out for them.

The flickering bugs trickled out of Simone's eye sockets and burst like a newborn from Carrie's glistening vagina. The dust was a mist now and it filled the basement like a steam bath.

"Soon," he said.

With Laura's torso gone, he had to wait for a replacement before he could build. He began thinking about other girls he'd loved, had made love to, or had ever had a crush on, as if willing them to die.

Only so many could still live around here.

He thought of strippers he'd wasted good money on and girls he had watched from afar and purposefully brushed up against in crowded places. He even thought of celebrities and women in nudie magazines.

He paced and cracked his knuckles. He was so eager and so ready. The girls were ready too. The time was now.

Make us one, they said.

In his mind's eye a creature of holy elegance floated in a sea of red dust and spread its many arms out like wings of death. Simone, Carrie, Amy, and Laura all fused together in an abstract shrine with extra limbs. He longed for its embrace.

Then a thought hit him like a sledgehammer. He thought of one particular woman's delicate frame, her clear skin and adorable, brown eyes. The smell of roses flared his nostrils and his body went slack with relief and he fell into a trance of peace as the flies swarmed in the mist.

"The choice is made," he told them.

Sarah had called out sick and the extra workload caused Tiffany to work later than usual. She was closing up by herself and she had to count down the till after she finished moving the flowers to the cooler and watering the plants. So late shoppers wouldn't annoy her by trying to get in, she left only a single light on. She put in her headphones and swept the floor, occasionally dancing with the broom, spinning it clumsily in her hands and letting off steam from the stress of a short-staffed workday. The music pumped in her head, rocking her into another world altogether.

She didn't hear the glass of the back door shatter. The new Taylor Swift was pulsing and she was shaking her hips as she pushed the broom back and forth with the beat. She raised the volume and began to sing along, planting the broom, using it as a microphone. Then she spun, and when she opened her eyes she saw the shape of the man in the dark. A jolt of fear ripped through her. She removed her headphones so fast that the whole player fell to the floor and shattered. She held the broom out in front of her like she was trying to shoo a cat.

The man stepped out of the shadows and, recognizing him, she felt a moment of relief.

It didn't last.

Somehow the scalpel shined even in the darkness.

Chapter Twenty-Two

After Jessica showered, they cleaned the wounds on her back and covered them with gauze to stop the bleeding. All in all, it hadn't been that bad. She was sliced and bruised, but she didn't think they would scar. The black eye and the cut in her bottom lip seemed worse to her. Jessica looked at herself in the mirror of her private bathroom. Her eyes were still dilated, but she felt the buzz of the dope wearing off. The pain intensified and she smiled.

Jessica reached over her shoulder and dug her hand beneath one of the bandages, ran her finger over the cut. It was still fresh and moist. She took her fingernail and dug into the wound, twisting deeper than the wound itself, puncturing her tissue further. She shuddered with delight, for the pain was sweet. It was a fresh gift and she knew it was changing her.

She was glad the drugs were wearing off. The sound of that buzzing was bothering her. It sounded like flies, but she couldn't see any in the room. The only strange thing she saw was the red dust that settled in small patches on her body even though she had just showered. It was as if her freckles were flaking off. She brushed at it, but it just kept regenerating, like dandruff.

She rubbed her finger in the wound again and when she withdrew it she brought it to her mouth and sucked the blood. The salty, coppery flavor was divine. She understood why Kandi had slurped it with fever. Billy had forced it out of her as if it too was an orgasm, and in a way, for her, it was. Blood had become her cum and she wanted to give the whole world a facial.

"You are a goddess," she told the mirror. "And you haven't even peaked yet."

"I need to know what's next," Kandi said. "Everything's getting crazier. If I can't be filled in, I'm walking."

Rutger fired up his cigar and it burned like a tiny sun in the blue light of the swimming pool. They were both submerged up to their waists. Kandi had gotten him alone and she wasn't backing down this time. He'd known this was coming. Her performances had become more lackluster and it wasn't entirely the booze's fault. She wasn't disgusted like so many other actors came to be—she was scared. There was stress behind her eyes that he hadn't seen before in all the years he had known her, not even when they had gone on wild coke binges to keep them going when they had to finish films on time and under budget.

But, frightened or not, she still hadn't bowed out. She wanted to be a part of this even though she had become nervous and apprehensive. Plus, there was all that fucking money. She knew she'd be losing out if she walked, because it would greatly damage the course of the film to derail the plot by having her simply disappear from it.

"To be honest," he said, "I'm not sure what's next. I'm waiting for Javier. He says he has something special."

"I'm worried, Rutger; for all of us. I feel like something is taking over, something . . . *evil.* When we do those shoots it's like I'm no longer myself. This animal sort of takes over and I don't return to normal until it's done."

"It's just the nature of the work. It awakens things inside of us that we were never even aware of. That's why they sell. These films bring out the monster in us all, even the viewers."

"But we're up to our necks in it," she said. "I think the deeper we sink the worse it's going to be. I think it might leave us permanently stained."

"You mean mentally? Like it will make us psychopaths or something?"

"Yes. Not just in our minds but in our souls. Like a curse."

He looked out into the night, the blue light of the pool rippling across his face and shoulders.

"I always took you for an atheist," he said.

"I am. I'm not talking about religion. I'm talking about our very humanity, and maybe even our lives."

He took another long puff, thinking about what he would say next. He had to assure her and lure her back in at the same time. He put his hand on her shoulder, squeezed a little.

"Kandi, baby, we all have our doubts when things get this intense. Many a time I thought of calling it quits but the art pulled me back in, and the money didn't hurt either. I've tried to keep things positive, because in the end this film will mean very good things for you. But if you break your contract and bail out now, I won't be the only one who is disappointed. The man behind the funding will be as well. He and his associates, I mean. And I don't know how much I could calm them down once they got angry. They are not the kind of men you want to be unhappy with you, Kandi. I certainly don't want that for either of us."

He wasn't trying to threaten and he certainly wasn't lying. He just had to put all the cards on the table. She was already in too deep, and the only way out was to go all the way through to the other side. He watched her process this new information as her shoulders dropped and she sank up to her neck in the water.

"When will we be finished?" she asked.

One of the other cabins nearby was having its roof redone and the repairman left the ladder out even when he wasn't working on it. Toby carried it over one shoulder as he made his way around the lake. Thunder groaned overhead; lightning hid in clouds that blocked all light from the moon. The shadows were thick and Toby welcomed their cloak. He had brought a flashlight just in case, but he didn't want to use it yet and give himself away. He also brought his pocketknife—again, just in case. He hoped that it too would go unused.

He was already shaking a little and he wasn't sure if it was from fear or anger, or both. Something told him that the pornographers wouldn't be as forgiving about him breaking in this time. He hoped to get into the property and then walk the perimeter to peek in the windows. If he could just find Jessica maybe he could get her attention somehow and lure her outside. He didn't have a solid plan after that. He just held fast to the hope that she would want to come with him.

Toby thought about all the things he might say and realized that if he had to tell her he loved her to get her to come with him, he would. He was surprised to discover that it wouldn't be a lie. He did love her. It wasn't until jealousy and worry came into the picture that it really dawned on him, and perhaps those were shallow routes to love, but he cared for her more than he had realized. He was her boyfriend and it was high time he treated her like more than a friend with benefits. Maybe there was still a chance for them. He wished that he could turn back the clock and stop them from ever going near that mansion, but what was done was done. Now they would have to try and put that behind them if they could. It would be difficult, but not impossible.

When he reached the gate Toby followed it around to the back of the house, ducking behind the bushes, keeping on the balls of his feet and making sure the ladder didn't show or crash into anything. He heard Rutger and Kandi talking in the pool but didn't hear Jessica. He came back to the side of the house and looked up at the towering windows. The curtains were drawn with dim light glowing behind the cloth. He gently placed the ladder on the gate and climbed up, his muscles tight in his straining stealth.

Once up, he straddled the gate and pulled the ladder end over end, placed it on the other side, and climbed down. He landed and collapsed the ladder. It made a metallic rattle. It wasn't loud, but he winced anyway. He slid it under the hedges for safekeeping and moved to the side of the house to get a better look through the windows.

There was a crack in the curtains of the first one and looking through it he could make out a low lamp on a nightstand. He saw a woman walk past, but she moved too quickly for him to tell if it was Jessica. Kandi was out back, but he didn't know if it was the fluffer or the boom operator or another porn star that had been brought in. He decided not to risk it until he could get another glimpse or two. He waited, but the woman did not pass by again.

He moved on to the next window and realized it was a different room. The curtains were opened wider here and the room appeared to be empty. He pushed on the window. It was unlocked. He slid it upward, listened to the silence for a moment, and then made his way inside.

Chapter Twenty-Three

Tiffany was even more beautiful naked.

Harold had slit her throat to keep her as undamaged as possible. Then he had taken her out the backdoor to the alley where the hearse was parked and placed her in back. She was still warm, so he put her up on the slab and had sex with her. It felt so good, the flesh still alive, he only lasted a few quick thrusts before popping off. He cleaned himself up and then began draining her blood with the aspirator. He was taking off her left arm when he heard the elevator coming down. Panic sent him into a frenzied dash. He pulled a sheet over Tiffany and grabbed another one to hide his collection. Simone's face was still smiling at him as he covered it. There were only a few of the strange red flies in the air and they seemed to sense his distress. Some flew down into his pockets while others hid in his ears and nostrils.

The door opened and his sister Maude came waddling out, glowering.

"Why the hell do you insist on working at this hour?" she asked.

"What are you doing here?"

"I manage this place, Harold. Have you forgotten?"

"This is *my* part of the business! Get out!"

"I need something, and I'll go where I want to go."

"This is *my* basement. You shouldn't disturb me during the artistic process."

"Give it a rest, Harold. You're not Picasso, you're an undertaker."

"My work brings in the customers."

"The grim reaper does that."

"You know what I mean."

He turned away from her and crossed his arms.

"Jesus Christ," Maude said. "You'd think we were still in junior high, the way you act. *Stay out of my room! No sisters allowed!*"

"Do not mock me."

Inside his skull he felt the flies buzzing, deafening like an attacked hornet's nest.

"Calm down. I just need a damn wrench. The sink is clogged again in the women's bathroom."

She went to the standing tool chest.

"Don't mess them up," he said. "They're all organized and sometimes I need the right tool right away or the body can collapse."

"Well, I doubt you'll be needing a wrench anytime soon."

She grabbed it, closed the chest, and walked back to the elevator.

"You need a girlfriend, Harold. You're starting to get a little nutty down here."

He put Tiffany's limbs aside and began working on her skull. It was not quite as perfect as Laura's, but it would do. She had good bone structure, and besides, the hair and eyes were just what he wanted. He trimmed the edges of her face and then, with care, rolled away the flesh just as he had done with

Simone. Tiffany's face, while pretty, had no place in this work of art, though he didn't want to simply dispose of it. It was too lovely for that. She had been his first and only kill, and in a way that made her as special as any lover, perhaps even more special. He wanted the face that had first attracted him to her to be with him forever, so he took the rolled up meat and put the whole thing into his mouth. He began to chew on it as if it were a strip of cold cuts. It was bloody and rich like roast beef, but not as salty as the nitrate-pumped deli meat Maude always bought. He wolfed it down and licked the blood from his lips.

Now it was time to make his masterpiece.

He uncovered the collection and placed Simone's face over Tiffany's skull. He placed both Amy's and Laura's legs near Tiffany's body where her vagina had been scooped out. He placed Carrie's vagina in the gap and then went for the pile of arms. He had Simone's and Laura's, having been unable to part with them, so he had four arms and four legs. He considered using one of each but decided it would be tacky to go the standard Frankenstein route. It would be droll at best and boring at worst. He wanted to make art here, not a fashion-shop mannequin. He decided that Simone's arms would go into the sockets where arms normally connected to the body. Laura's however would be attached at the back of the shoulders so they could serve as wings.

Like a fly's.

The legs would fan out from beneath the body like peacock feathers and just as beautiful. He thought it would be best to saw off the feet and put them on the opposing legs, switching limbs and directions. He had a lot of work to do, but passion was coursing through him with the fury of a tornado. His hands got to work, moving quickly, buzzing louder and louder as the tools twitched into the sweet, sweet flesh.

Chapter Twenty-Four

They put on their robes and came in from the pool. Rutger made them both a gin and tonic and they sat down on the sofa, Kandi petting Cougar. Her fur had a nice calming effect on Kandi, and the purring soothed her jangled nerves.

Just one or two more shoots, she told herself. *Then I'm heading back to L.A. to forget about this insane asylum. From now on I'm sticking to the online MILF bullshit. I don't care if my stardom has faded. I made some quality films in my time and no one can take that away from me.*

Billy walked in from the kitchen. She was surprised he was still there because he usually left with the crew after sets. Seeing him, she hoped that the crew was still around somewhere too. It would mean there would be another shoot tonight. Sore as she was, she was game to get it done.

"I'd like to get all of this over with as fast as possible," she said to both of them.

Billy sat down beside her and put his hand on her damp thigh. She didn't like that, so she crossed her legs and slid it off.

"I agree with Kandi," Billy said. "I'm getting less and less comfortable with this stuff."

Rutger sipped his drink.

"You two surprise me," he said. "You seem into it when we're filming. You must be better actors than I ever knew. You could have won an Oscar for that last take, Billy boy."

"It must have been the drugs," he said. "I've never been like that before. I'm not too happy with myself."

Now it was Kandi who wanted to reach out to him. She had misunderstood what his previous touch had meant. She put her hand on his shoulder in solidarity.

"I'm not happy either," she said. "Didn't you feel like you weren't even yourself?"

"Yeah, I felt like I went out of my head."

"So you want to bow out?" Rutger asked.

"It's not that," Billy said. "I just want to wrap it up. I know we've got one more shoot tonight. Will this be the end of my involvement?"

"I'm not sure yet. It depends on what Javier brings for us. He says he has something good, so I'll have to decide if it's good enough for a finale. A climax ain't just a money shot you know."

A man stepped out of the hallway and at first Kandi thought it was Ben. Then as he approached the light she recognized him as Toby, Jessica's boyfriend.

"Where is she?" the teenager asked.

His face was hard and determined, his body tense like a dog ready to attack. He even bared his teeth like one.

Rutger stood and put up his hands. Kandi stood too.

"Easy, buddy," Rutger said. "Just calm down and take a seat."

"I asked you a question," Toby said.

He came down the steps into the living room, closing the distance to Rutger. Kandi watched Toby, hoping he wouldn't do anything foolish but also glad that he was intervening. He must care about Jessica, and that girl needed to get out of this even more than she or Billy. She was young. She had her whole life ahead of her. If Jessica wanted to spend it in the adult film industry that was fine, but she didn't need all this violence on her soul. Jessica was getting more sadistic too. Kandi had seen the bloodlust when her eyes went red and she'd gone into the dark place within. The girl needed to be rescued from herself before she was lost to it forever.

"Look, kid," Rutger said, "what was your name again?"

"Toby! Now look—I play football and I won't hesitate to take you down. I'm gonna ask you one more time. Where is she?"

Kandi heard another door opening down the hall. His yelling had roused someone. They all turned as Jessica walked out, still naked for whatever reason. Her eyes were large and black like two eight balls forced into the sockets. No one said a word as she walked down the steps with a big grin on her face that threatened to reopen her split lip.

"Toby," she said. "You came back!"

She went to him and took him in her arms. As he hugged Jessica, Kandi watched him touch the bandages that had gone pink. The pressure of his hands made some of them bloom with blood again. He turned her around and his face went the color of cottage cheese.

"Oh my god." He looked into her drugged, dilated eyes. "What did you bastards, do to her?"

Billy looked away, guilt deflating his body. Kandi hoped Toby wouldn't notice, and he didn't. He was too busy giving Rutger the evil eye.

"You son of a bitch," Toby said.

"Take it easy there, Toby." Rutger stepped back.

Toby put Jessica behind him, shielding her, and drew a knife from his pocket. He flicked it open and held it toward Rutger. Billy stood up as Kandi stepped between the two men. She felt confident that the boy wouldn't hurt her, and she didn't want him to do something he'd regret from behind bars. Besides, they were close to Rutger's den where he kept his guns on display, loaded.

"Don't," she said. "It was just an S&M scene. She wanted to do it and she's going to be okay."

"I'm taking her out of here."

"That's fine," Kandi said. "No one is going to stop you."

She saw a flash of headlights pass across the windows.

Oh no.

"Just take her," Kandi said. "Go out the back and get her out of here now."

"He loves me," Jessica said deliriously, hanging on Toby like he was a jungle gym. "He really *loves* me, Kandi."

"Yes, I can see that he does. Why don't you go with him now, honey, okay?"

"But I want to finish our movie."

She sounded like a sleepy child who wanted to stay up.

Kandi nodded. "You can do it later."

"Like hell," Toby said. "We're going back home."

"I didn't get my money yet," Jessica said. "There's more to film. I'm gonna be a big star, Toby. You've gotta see."

Kandi heard a car door close, but Toby seemed too preoccupied with his anger to notice it.

Damn it, kid; just get out of here before it's too late!

"You drugged her," Toby said. "You drugged her to get her to do what you wanted. Then you cut her and busted her face up, you sick fucks! I'm going to the police, Rutger! You're not going to get away with this!"

The front door opened and Kandi felt her heart fall as Javier entered with something big wrapped in a trash bag slung over his shoulder. Seeing Toby, he dropped it with a thud. Toby spun around and held the knife out in front of him.

"Don't come any closer," Toby said.

Javier closed the door and stepped into the living room.

"I said don't move!"

But Javier kept moving. He did not flinch as he walked up the steps and stopped when his chest pressed against the tip of the knife. Toby's arm began to shake and Kandi believed he had stopped breathing.

"Stab me, *esé*," Javier said. "If you've got the *cajones*."

Toby held the knife in place, but aside from his trembling, he didn't move. Jessica was still in a smiling stupor. And Javier's face remained a slate.

"Come on," Javier said. "Kill me."

"This young man wants to take our new leading lady," Rutger said. "He wants to take her to the police station."

"Is that right?" Javier did not take his eyes off Toby.

Toby turned to look at Jessica and it was all the time Javier needed. With both hands he grabbed Toby's wrist that held the knife. Kandi shuddered when she heard it snap. Toby howled and Javier silenced him with a blow to the solar plexus, knocking the wind from his lungs. Toby fell and Javier grabbed his head, slamming the teen's face into his knee twice. Toby collapsed with a gushing, broken nose.

In a daze, Jessica leaned down next to him, ran her fingers in the blood, and licked them clean. Then she ran her hand through his hair and kissed his ear.

"Let's fuck," she whispered.

Toby felt the cuffs snap onto his wrists.

"Just until we finish the movie," Rutger said.

The three of them were alone in the small room. Thick rope around his chest tied Toby to one of the kitchen chairs and his arms were around the chair's back. Binds held his ankles to the wooden legs. His nose was backing blood into his throat and his wrist had gone numb. Every nerve in his body twanged, the fear making his hairs stand on end.

Javier grimaced. "You said he was going to the police."

"He's not going to do that, right kid?" Rutger said.

Toby didn't answer.

"Your little girlfriend consented to everything," Rutger said. "You've got no case."

"Then why are you tying me up?"

"Because we don't need police interrupting our movie. Besides, you don't want them here now. My associate might have busted you up, sure, but you were breaking and entering, remember?"

Toby sighed. The scumbag was right.

"Trust me, kid, we'll be done shooting soon and you and Jess can drive on home, five grand richer. You get your girl back, we get our movie, and everybody makes money. So turn that frown upside down, will ya? We're looking at a happy ending here."

Kandi walked Jessica out to the deck alone.

The girl was playing with Toby's knife.

They'd taken him behind closed doors, and when Kandi tried to join them, to make sure Toby would be okay, Rutger asked her to tend to Jessica and assured her the kid wouldn't be hurt any further.

"Toby's not going to leave without me, is he?" Jessica asked.

"Not from what I saw, honey."

"I mean to school. He's going to take me to Knoxville with him."

They reached the poolside and Kandi looked down at the water. Rutger liked his swims cool so he had turned the heater off earlier when Kandi had gotten out. She shoved Jessica, but the girl snatched her wrist and so both of them splashed into the pool. The temperature had dropped with the oncoming storm and the water felt even colder than it had all week. Kandi jolted up and clutched her arms around her. Jessica did the same.

"Jesus!" Jessica shivered.

She rubbed her eyes and already Kandi thought she could see some sense returning to them. Jessica looked around like she had just awoken from a weird dream, and perhaps she had.

"What the hell, Kandi?"

"You needed to sober up."

"I was coming down."

"Not fast enough. Do you even know what just happened?"

Jessica's brow furrowed in thought.

"Fuck," she said.

A large bandage floated by and Jessica raised her hand out of the water. It still held the knife.

"Oh, fuck," she said. "Toby."

"That's right, honey."

"Is he okay?"

"Javier roughed him up."

"Yeah, I remember."

"Listen, I think if we just get through this last shoot Rutger will let you guys go. He's a reasonable man and he's my friend. But you have to promise no cops."

"What?"

"No cops, Jess. You have to make sure Toby doesn't get the police involved. These are illegal films. The men who finance them are dangerous, you understand?"

Jessica had started looking at the knife again.

"Wake up!" Kandi shook her.

"Okay, okay."

"One more shoot. Let's just hammer through it, no matter how fucked up it is."

"You don't have to tell me, Kandi. I've been on board since day one and I'm not gonna stop until I reach the top."

Kandi let her go and pushed her hair away from her face. The girl's eyes were back to normal, but there was still something wild and disturbing behind them.

She hoped it wasn't too late.

In the slaughter room, Javier dumped the torso out onto the slab and stepped back. Rutger's mouth dropped. "You weren't kidding," he said.

Rutger bent down to get a better look at her. Even without limbs she was a very pretty woman. He poked her as if he couldn't even believe she was real, half-expecting her to jump up and say *boo*! He felt sick and excited at the same time. This was the finishing touch that the film needed, for sure, and with two of his actors having serious doubts and the other one's boyfriend's tied up down the hall, even Rutger was now eager to get the picture in the can. He wanted to finish it off for editing. Then the maids could clean the house from top to bottom and get the foul stench of gore out, as well as that goddamn dust.

"You want me to dope up the stars?" Javier asked.

"No more drugs. I want them wide-awake for the finale."

"What about the boy? We need to do something with him."

Rutger stood. "No, wait a second—"

"He knows too much," Javier said. "He's already threatened with going to the pigs."

Rutger regretted sharing that information. "The kid won't go to the cops. Even if he does we have her consenting on camera."

"Vic won't like it if we have to explain anything to some pigs. We don't need their snouts sniffing around."

"He broke in twice, Javier. If he goes to the cops, he goes down too. Jessica *wants* to be a porn star for Christ's sakes. She's not going to let her boyfriend jeopardize the connections she's made. Sure, she started in the underground, but she could have a promising career in the mainstream. I could introduce her to people. These kids have everything to gain if they play their cards right, so don't worry, the kid was just blowing off steam."

Javier still looked angry, but he always looked that way.

"Trust me," Rutger said. "I've been in this business for forty years, and if there is one thing I know it's that money changes minds. Money forgives all."

Chapter Twenty-Five

In the dark of his sanctuary, Harold reclined in his swivel chair and watched the crimson ballet that played out before him. The bottoms of the flies had swelled to cherries and the red dust squirted out of them, propelling them through the darkness and illuminating it. The whole basement glowed like a photography dark room.

Harold was nude and his penis was erect, engorged to its maximum fullness, but his lover wasn't touching him. She didn't need to. Her radiance, which filled the rear wall with brilliant, pink light, was all he needed to be aroused. Writhing, his postmortem creation swelled and deflated again and again like a giant, gleaming heart, a monstrosity of paralyzing beauty.

"My masterpiece," he said.

His cock swayed back and forth and pre-cum rose from the hole.

We've always loved you, Harold.

The walls began to shudder, sending small, blinding cracks through them like hot lightning. The swarm was buzzing louder now, an industrial symphony.

There were hundreds of them.

They smacked into his skin and spun through his hair. More of them came forward, spilling from his lover's mouth in a red geyser. It looked as if she was vomiting blood and the sight made him ejaculate.

"I love you," he said. "I love you all."

We're hungry, Harold. So hungry.

Maude came into the funeral home and shook the rain from her umbrella. She hung up her slicker, cursed, and took off her boots. Outside, the sky had opened in a furious downpour and her cuffs were soaked and her face was just as gloomy as the weather.

She turned on the foyer light.

God, he keeps it dark in here. You'd think he was Dracula.

She walked into the main lobby, turning on more lights as she went. Seeing her brother's car still parked out front she rolled her eyes and wondered if he would ever regain some semblance of life. As much as he frustrated her, he was still her brother, and she hated seeing him rotting in a basement among a pile of corpses. He had become so withdrawn, defensive, and secretive. She wondered if he may have a mental illness and wished she could figure out a way to get him to see a psychiatrist without him exploding at her just for suggesting he might need help. She had promised her parents that she would take care of their troubled only son, just as she had promised to take care of the family business.

Business was good; Harold, not so much.

Maude decided that as long as he was going to be there all night, she might as well bring him something to eat. Maybe she couldn't keep him mentally healthy, but she could at least keep him physically healthy. In the plastic bag she had fried rice for herself and a dish of moo goo gai pan for Harold—his favorite—and a box of eggrolls for them to share.

She walked down the corridor and lifted the latch on the elevator. She took note of the red dust that filled it and knew she would have to have a talk with Glenn about tidiness. She would not stand for filth. On the way down, she noticed a strange, pungent odor in the air. It was a bad, organic stink, like body odor or shit. When she reached the bottom and opened the door, the waft hit her and she had to lean on the wall.

The smell was rot.

She gagged on it and had to cough it out. Putting her shirt over her mouth and nose she looked up, and immediately found the source.

She dropped the bag.

The thing was on the wall, but it did not seem to be attached. The arms were spread out like a perverted statue of Vishnu and the legs slithered like tentacles in the uncanny, pink light that seemed to throb from beneath the thing's torn and mangled flesh. The vagina was opening and closing as if giving birth to some unseen infant, and she could tell it did not belong to that torso originally but had been crudely mashed into the pelvis and locked in place by surgical staples.

But the worst part was the face.

It was crooked on the skull, held secure by stitches that oozed and fizzed with yellow pus. The eyes, sunken in the hollow pits of the face, stared at Maude, burning a flame of terror into her soul that made her wet herself.

She walked backward, retreating from the monster, unable to look away from the grotesquery. When she felt the arm close upon her throat she tried to scream, but she couldn't take in enough air to do so. She pulled on the arm and managed to break free, stumbling into the worktable, overturning it, and falling with it to the floor.

Harold's naked body lunged and he landed on her, thrashing. His hand went around her throat again, his legs gripping her sides and his erection jutting into her stomach. His other hand came up with the aspirator as she reached up and clawed at his face, tearing each of his cheeks with her nails. He didn't seem to feel it. He actually *smiled* at her. His eyes were as red as rubies, glowing, changing. He twisted her head to one side and the aspirator came down, stabbing into the side of her neck, blunt and intrusive, and the pain shook her body like an electric shock. The tip went all the way into her throat and she instantly began choking on her own blood. It rose and pushed out of her mouth and nose, and the rest of it came pumping out of the aspirator in a smooth jet, splashing onto her brother's arms as swarms of flies came whizzing out of every hole in his head.

Chapter Twenty-Six

There was a fierce energy in the room. Everyone was sober and yet their sheer adrenaline made their eyelids twitch and kept their fingers cracking their knuckles incessantly. Even the crew was on edge. Tye seemed on the verge of walking out the door. Ben and Mia both wore grim faces. In the director's chair, Rutger leaned forward, tense. His eyes were hard and cool like a glacier. Next to him, Javier stood with a smug smile that made Jessica a little uncomfortable.

She was propped up in the chair with the stirrups. She wore a tight vinyl outfit, cherry red with zippers and studs, and a matching pair of knee-high boots. She had a vibrator in her hand and was ready to go. She kept checking it, thinking it might be on because she kept hearing an annoying buzzing. But the vibrator was turned off. She found herself digging in her ears and looking up at the florescent lights, unsure if the buzzing was external or internal.

Kandi stood next to Billy, both of them in black leather, right in front of the slab where a big, indistinguishable lump was covered by a sheet.

"This is our last, full shoot," Rutger said. "After this, all we'll need to do is a couple of scripted dialogue scenes, but no more sex or . . . *surprises.*"

Jessica sighed. It bothered her that Toby couldn't be in on the show to at least watch her perform, but she knew very well that he wouldn't be able to handle it. They had enough to discuss and consider once this was over without him witnessing the finale. She wasn't happy about him being locked in another room either, but she understood Rutger's reasoning. The film was so close to completion. Nothing could stand in the way of it. It was art, and art cannot be compromised.

"Roll camera," Rutger said. "Sound."

Ben snapped the clapperboard.

"Action."

Jessica turned on the vibrator and Tye zoomed in on her while Ben focused his camera on Kandi kissing Billy. Mia swung the boom low, but seemed hesitant to get too close. Her face had darkened. This scene went on for a few minutes, then Kandi went down on Billy and he put his hands on her head. Jessica faked an orgasm just so she could finish with the chair and join her costars. She hated playing with herself in a scene. She wanted to be in on every second of the action. Kneeling down beside Kandi, they took turns blowing Billy and sucking on his scrotum.

The lights overhead began to flicker and the room grew chilly. Goose bumps rose on her flesh and Jessica scooted even closer to Kandi just for her body warmth. As she did, she felt grains of sand grind into her knees and she looked down to see that they were kneeling in a red sandpit that had not been there a moment ago. With each flicker of the lights the buzzing seemed to grow louder. She listened closer and realized it was coming from the lump on the slab.

Enticed, Jessica stood up, took Billy by his stiff dick, and led him over to where the lump sat waiting. Kandi followed and the three of them each took a side. Jessica grabbed hold of the sheet and licked her lips, knowing that whatever would be good enough for their grand finale would be something that would take her to new heights of sexual ecstasy. She wanted to inflict and receive anguish again, both mental and physical. She wanted to test the limits of her own humanity and dignity, to break through to another plane of unabashed pleasure and writhe in its hot rivers. Her blood pulsed in anticipation, her heart pounding against her ribcage.

This is it.

Pulling back the sheet slowly, savoring the reveal, Jessica was the first to see the body's face. It was elegant, like a model's in a makeup ad. She pulled the shroud a little farther to see that the arms were missing, and then lower, seeing that the legs were as well, a quadriplegic Venus.

Holy shit. Not just a dead body, a cut-down one to boot.

Billy's jaw dropped and Kandi took a few steps back. She had a look on her face of abject horror and tears brewed in her eyes. Jessica tried to get her attention, to smile at her and assure her that everything was going to be all right. This was their last shoot. If Kandi could just hold tight it would all be over for her very soon. She could collect her fat paycheck, fly back to California, and never again have to involve herself in something like this; something she clearly couldn't handle the way Jessica could.

With Billy's cock still in her hand, Jessica bent over the torso, resting on it sideways while still standing, and she guided Billy into her. His erection was deflating, so she took his hands and put them to her tits and started grinding on him the way he liked. Billy took a deep breath and started pinching her nipples, as if he was starting to get his head in the game. He thrust back.

Jessica moaned as he fucked her and ran her hands across the jagged, meaty nubs where the torso's limbs should be. She sucked on its cold, gray nipples. Licking her fingers she put two digits in the dead vagina and one in its anus, then began pumping it, rocking the shocker. The lights flickered faster, creating a strobe-light effect, and the hue went from piss yellow to a soft pink that morphed into a red that matched the sand beneath her boots. Billy fucked her harder, his cock getting nice and big, but Kandi had yet to move.

"Come to me," Jessica told Kandi.

She clicked her tongue at her and continued to stare her down.

"Look at her," Kandi said to Rutger. "Look at her eyes."

"Get in there," Rutger said. "One take, remember? We're almost done, baby."

He gave her a nudge and she went to Jessica. Her hesitation was obvious. She was trying to control her breathing. The corpse clearly disturbed her more than anything they had done so far, but Jessica knew how Kandi worked. She was always a little spooked at first, until she got into it, and then the sickness—the white-hot rage—would take over her, just as it always did to Jessica. Her eyes would roll in her head and she'd bare her teeth as if she were growing fangs. Her hair would whip in the blood and her lips would pucker up to the steaming gore. All she needed was a little encouragement.

As Kandi got closer, Jessica took her hands in hers and guided her down to the torso. They were both leaning on it now and Jessica put her tongue in Kandi's mouth. She clutched the sides of her head, sucking her inward, hoping her passion would transfer over to Kandi and make her inner animal awaken. Their tongues wrestled like snakes and when their mouths separated, Billy exited Jessica and walked around the table to Kandi. Still wet from Jessica, he was able to get his cock into Kandi's ass with ease. Jessica watched as Kandi's eyes closed and Jessica caught a faint glimpse of the pleasure she'd been waiting to see on Kandi's face. Humping Kandi, Billy leaned down and started kissing Jessica.

They continued this basic sex for a while and then Jessica got up and went to the end of the slab where the corpse's head was. She leaned in and slid her tongue into its mouth and the moment she did she felt several small things enter her own mouth and begin spinning inside of it. Jessica tried to pull back, but glue-like mucus had risen from the corpse's lips and stuck her there. She gagged on the things as they spun against her cheeks and flew down her throat.

Bugs, she realized.

They swarmed inside Jessica and she was forced to swallow. Some of them came up her throat and out her nose as she heaved. She put her hands on the slab and pushed until her lips tore from the corpse's with such force that she fell on her butt.

"Jessica?" Kandi looked down at her.

But Jessica couldn't reply. The swarm was spreading through her. She could feel them flying around inside of her lungs and wiggling their way into her brain. She coughed and hacked, her body warming. She sneezed and when she drew her hand from her nose she immediately thought it was filled with blood, but looking closer she could see that her palm held three flies. They shined like red Christmas lights.

Suddenly a rush overcame her like a freight train, barreling through her soul. She felt herself being elevated by it, as if she were levitating. The force brought her to her feet and she let its warmth bathe her. It was like swimming in hot semen and being kissed by a thousand tongues. It was beyond titillating, beyond erotic. Her whole body quivered in a thunderous orgasm and she felt the bloodlust boil inside her, a powerful volcano screaming. She felt lethal. She could smell Kandi's cunt and Billy's asshole from where she stood, as well as the crew's body odor beneath their perfumes and deodorant. She could taste the tiny particles of their flesh that danced with the dust mites in the air. She was entirely aware of every inch of her body. Her skin flushed and rippled over her muscles. Her teeth and fingernails grew a little longer as her freckles multiplied and her hair curled into rippling waves.

The force of the bloodlust became all encompassing.

She wanted more.

She *needed* more.

Turning to Billy, she smacked him across the face, hard and nasty. Before he could register what had happened, she raked his chest, tearing his pecs. He pulled out of Kandi and came at her with his fist held high.

"Hit me!" she cried.

His knuckles slammed into her, catching the side of her head, causing her vision to go to stars. She cackled, grabbed his ass, and raked it too. He retaliated by grabbing her pussy lips and twisting them. She grew wetter, took his hair in her hands, and dragged him over to the corpse. With a newfound strength, she mashed Billy's face down into the corpse's purpled vagina. She kept one hand on the back of his head, raised the elbow of her free arm, and dropped it hard into the corpse's stomach. A mix of mortuary chemicals, bodily fluids, and rotted bits of flesh squirted into Billy's mouth.

"Lick it up!" Jessica pushed his face deeper into the oozing hole and elbow-dropped the corpse a second time. Billy vomited, but she held him there, letting him choke on the bile. Mia groaned at the sight. Tye turned away from his camera, gagging, but Rutger had an awed look on his face that made Jessica proud. Javier was in the corner, rubbing his stiff dick beneath his jeans. Jessica's laughter filled the room.

She released Billy's head and took a step back. He got up and the fury in his eyes excited her. He lunged and slammed her head against the wall.

"Bitch!"

He bent Jessica over the corpse and began beating her. He punched her kidneys and smacked her ass raw. She pissed herself from the pain, but it was rocketing her into the same plane of pleasure she'd felt when her back had been shredded. Billy took his engorged cock and forced it deep into her ass. He began rage-fucking her and he took a fistful of her hair and snapped her neck backward while continuing to beat her with his free hand.

When she opened her eyes, Jessica saw that Kandi was fingering herself just inches from her face. She had the look of bloodlust about her now and Jessica knew that she wasn't alone. Her sister in sickness had returned, and she delighted when Kandi's pussy reached her lips.

Reaching up, Billy snagged the chain that dangled from the ceiling. A meat hook was attached to the end of it and he gripped it hard, bring it down as he kept fucking her. At first she was disappointed that he hadn't stabbed her with it, but then she realized what he was doing. He ground the hook into the corpse's stomach, twisting and turning until he had ripped it open and exposed the guts.

The bloodlust had possessed them all now.

In a bit of revenge, Billy smashed her face into the guts and Jessica sucked and lapped at them as the rubbery intestines squirmed beneath her like a squid. She began chewing as more orgasms shook her body with little earthquakes and she separated the lower intestines from the stomach. A pungent stench filled her nostrils and she drank down the putrid swill.

Kandi moved around to Billy and began kissing him and playing with his balls. He exited Jessica's ass, pushed Kandi down, and put his dick in her mouth. She throated him with fervor and he fucked her face with a lion's roar. Jessica got up, dragging the length of intestine with her teeth, and she slapped Kandi's face away and took Billy's cock. It was like stone. She took the end of the intestine and slid it down over Billy's cock like it was a condom and she jerked him off. Kandi slid back underneath him and let his balls fill her mouth as she crammed her nose into his asshole. Jessica got to her knees and stroked him with the guts, and just as he was about to climax she took him out and put both his cock and the length of intestines up to her open mouth, both spewing across her face.

Chapter Twenty-Seven

Fluid gel, red and alive.

The blob was omnipotent.

It writhed upon every wall and made cyclones of the ceiling and floor. It stuck to the soles of Harold's feet and climbed up the insides of his legs like wet weeds. It fell from the ceiling and spilled over his head, down into his mouth, and back out across his bare chest. It coated his genitals and slathered his back in its hot, crimson goo.

Harold heard the masterpiece, *The Goddess*—she burped as she snapped Maude's bones, pulling his sister deeper into the slime. He watched her absorbing his sister's limbs and decapitated head into her thrashing, contorted hull, and the romantic in him gushed.

The Goddess's love filled him with a soft, pink light that hugged his soul like a mother would cradle a child. She had made the basement her womb to have and to hold him in, and he was her treasure and she was his everything. The hole he'd felt in his heart was now filled, the combination of all his many loves fulfilling him more completely than any single one of them had been able to do on their own.

"I love you," he said. "I love you, my darlings."

He felt his eyes beginning to expand and push their way

out of the sockets. The pressure of the insects was forcing them out, but he knew now that he no longer needed them. He reached up with both hands and clenched his wet eyeballs, pulling them further until they were out of his head, and then he gave them one full tug, ripping them out with the neural tissue and severing them from the optic nerves. He licked at the blood that dribbled from the sockets and felt the flies cover his face, neck, and shoulders. They stuck to the goo, fusing to him, and they just kept coming, caking him in their throbbing bodies until they coated his entire body. They buzzed in a deafening chorus and when Harold opened his mouth to sing with them, a sound came out of him like a throat singer—vibrating, droning, nearly inhuman.

He was one with the flies now, and as The Goddess's many limbs coiled around him, their fingers and toes squirming into him, he knew that he would soon be one with her too.

Chapter Twenty-Eight

Sitting in the shower with her arms around her knees, Kandi cried and cried. She felt filthy, as if she had been raped, and yet she had only herself to blame. It was a self-violation. Her mind flashed with blazing memories of gore.

What has been done cannot be undone. You will carry this forever.

Each time the bloodlust had overtaken her it was worse: stronger and meaner. Its power was growing with each atrocity, feeding off of the abominations they created. She was in an absolute black state during the last shoot. Not only was she removed, she felt trapped inside of herself, as if she was a spectator watching herself from within her own body.

There was a dark presence here in the house, and Kandi could feel it germinating like a cancer. It was as if with each terrible and grotesque thing they did, the house became imbued with a malevolent sentience. She knew that the nightmare that would never stop haunting her was not of her own doing. She had been overpowered by the evil presence that had taken control of the shoots. It had manipulated all of them. Billy and Jessica had done the worst of it, but they too had been lost to the thrall of the evil. It was everywhere. It filled the house like a curse, powdering it with its strange, desert sand and insects. She was still in fear of it, for it was unscrupulous and sinister, and not to be trusted or ignored.

Her only solace now was that it was over. There would be no more sex scenes and no more horrors to send her back into the dark spiral. The madness was behind her. All they had to do was the stupid dialogue scenes, which wouldn't take long. Then she could go home without fear of Rutger's mobster employers hunting her down. She would leave with a purse bursting with cash, but that didn't matter as much anymore. She just wanted to leave and never look back.

Rutger slammed back the tumbler of scotch, his third in less than ten minutes. He had long thought that nothing could rattle him anymore, but he was wrong.

I have to get out of this business. I have made my final horror show.

He was pleased with the footage. The movie would be his greatest underground work, but he was more than happy to leave it at that. He knew it would be a smashing success. He knew the market. The sick assholes were going to go fucking apeshit. Vic and his associates would applaud the sales and they would be ready to throw an avalanche of cash at him for his next picture, but he knew now that he was finished, once and for all. His mind couldn't handle any more of this ghastly business and he worried that he might have already caused some permanent damage to his psyche. He didn't want to see revolting terrors every time he closed his eyes.

Already thinking disturbing thoughts, he was startled by Javier's voice behind him.

"You really are a genius, Mr. Malone. I knew you were good for a *gringo*, but up until now I was on the fence about the genius part. Not anymore."

Javier joined him at the bar and poured himself a shot of bourbon.

"We should celebrate," Javier said. "A little coke, a little tequila. I could call in some of the dirty girls for us."

"Thanks anyway, but I'm not in the mood for sex. After tonight, I don't know if I ever will be again."

Javier laughed.

"Not me. That was the hottest thing I've ever seen. That girl is insane! What's her name again? Jessica?"

"Yeah."

"She's gonna make our outfit rich!"

"Vic can draw her a contract," Rutger said. "I'm out. Kandi too."

He poured another drink. The scotch was good but somehow impotent at the moment.

"Are you nuts?" Javier asked. "You've got a blockbuster here."

"I'm old and worn out. I think it's time to retire."

Javier shook his head. "If you say so, Mr. Malone."

"We shoot some filler material and then it's *adiós*."

"What a shame. You waste your gift."

Rutger poured another. "Better to go out on top, right?"

Javier seemed disappointed.

"I wish I could make movies like you," he said. "I have so many great ideas."

As much as he struggled, Toby couldn't even shake the ropes a little loose. The cuffs dug into him, making his wrists ache, particularly the one he figured to be broken, given the hot river of pain that throbbed inside of it. He was hungry and he had to piss, but those were the least of his concerns.

How long have I been in here?

The heavy curtains blocked the windows and he couldn't tell if it was day or night. There was a weird redness in the air too, like a fog, and it seemed to be making him lightheaded and delirious. He feared that they might be gassing him; drugging him as they had done to Jessica.

Terror clawed its way through his skull.

Jessica was somewhere in the house, doing things he didn't want to think about. Worse still, things were being done to her. Thinking of her broken face and ripped open back, he felt the tears begin to fall. He was the big, strong football player, but he had failed her. As her boyfriend, he was supposed to protect her. He was supposed to be a man, fearless and unstoppable. But he wasn't fearless, and the Mexican had stopped him.

Toby wished he had stabbed him when he had the chance. He wished he had driven the blade right into his black heart. He should have at least put up a fight. His failure to act disgraced him. He felt like a total pussy.

He prayed that it would be the last humiliation he would endure within the walls of this hell house, but he doubted it. The worst was in no way behind him, no matter what the Mexican and Rutger said. He was their prisoner and he knew he wasn't going to be released easily, if they even let him go at all.

What awful things are they going to do to me?

Jessica felt them stirring.

They were everywhere—under her skin, swimming in her organs and blessing her with their burning. They swelled her breasts and made them lactate. She could feel them flickering in her womb and planting their maggot seeds in her bowels. It tickled her and she giggled. They were romancing her now, cooing at their new mommy, and she rubbed her belly and hummed for them, returning their love.

She brushed her hair in the mirror. It had grown longer and was now a darker, heavier red, almost ruby. With each stroke more of the scarlet dust sprinkled and floated about her like lava drifting in a lamp. She had many more freckles now too—not the brownish-orange ones she'd always had, but bright red ones she had initially taken for specs of the dust. It looked as if she had been soaking in the sun for days. Her flesh was now more red than white, as if the white parts were the freckles and not the other way around. Her eyes were bloodshot and she had become incredibly vascular, her arms bursting with veins as the flies traveled through them on blood rivers.

I am divine.

There was a knock at the door and hearing it her babies sunk deeper beneath the surface of her, burrowing down into hibernation until it was time for them to once again taste what she offered. Dissolving like water, her freckles receded back into her skin, leaving her with a pink sheen as if she had just stepped out of a scorching bath.

She didn't even have to go to the door to know who it was.

She could smell him.

"You still in there, Jess?" Rutger asked.

"I'm coming."

A moment later she opened the door and let him in. She wore only a towel.

"I just wanted to check on you," he said.

"I'm fine."

"You sure?"

"Yeah. I mean, why shouldn't I be?"

He crossed his arms and looked away.

"Well," he said. "That was an intense shoot we just did there."

"Oh," she said. "Did it not go well?"

"No, no," he said. "That's what we've been going for. It's just that, well . . . "

"What?"

"It's just that you went into it with such gusto, such *fervor*. Don't get me wrong, that was great for the scene, I just want to make sure you're feeling okay."

"I feel great."

He looked at her with concerned eyes. She appeared unfazed and he wondered what was really going on in the girl's mind.

"Are you sure?" he asked.

"Never felt better. I guess the whole thing just excited me."

A silence lingered there for a moment, stiff between them.

"Okay," he said. "We have a few non-sex scenes we need to do for filler, but otherwise we're good. We just have one small problem."

"What?"

"It's Kandi and Billy, they're . . . "

"Yes?"

"They've become . . . a little . . . *afraid* of you."

"Of me? Shit, after Kandi drank my blood and Billy pushed my face into that dead body's guts, they have the nerve to be afraid of me?"

"I think it's just your intensity," Rutger said. "Don't be offended."

"Fuck the two of them. He's nothing but a big cock and she's a washed-up has-been."

"We need them for the final scenes, Jess. Can you help me out?"

She rolled her eyes like the teenager she was.

"What? You want me to apologize to the candy asses?"

"No, that's not necessary. I think they just need to see that you're mellow now, that what happened during the shoot was an act, and nothing more."

She paused for a moment and then sighed, exasperated. "Fine, I'll do that for you. But what do I get?"

"What do you need?"

He thought about Toby locked away in another room.

"I want a deal," she said, grinning. "For more movies."

"That shouldn't be a problem, not with your looks and talent. You could even move up to the majors. I have connections."

"No," she said. "That's weak. Kid shit. I want more underground films—the pitch-black ones, the blood and guts."

He couldn't believe it; and yet, in her case, he could.

"You mean . . . "

"Yes. Gore, violence, sin. All of the pleasures I've tasted here. I want to make more of this art, Rutger. You've taught me what true art really is."

I'm so sorry, kid.

"Think it over, Jess. I know the money is good but—"

"Money can't buy what I've tasted."

"This business is very dangerous."

"That's half the thrill. You know that."

There was something strange in her voice. It had changed somehow, and now that he noticed it he also noticed the way her face had changed. Not just over the past few days, but just since he had entered the room. Her jaw seemed larger, like a man's, and when she wasn't speaking it hung slack, baring her teeth. Her gums were an unhealthy-looking maroon. He had attributed her bloodshot eyes to stress or possibly the drugs, but now he wondered if it wasn't part of something more sinister. She was even starting to intimidate *him* now.

"You'd get more famous in the big leagues," he said.

"I'm not interested. That's not the itch I need to scratch."

"Okay then. If that's what you want. My producers will be happy. They're gonna want you for a series after they see this one, I assure you."

Chapter Twenty-Nine

Glenn unlocked the door and stepped inside. Already he could see what Ms. Ruben was talking about. Some sort of red dirt was all over the floor of the lobby, like a bunch of kids had ripped open thousands of Kool-Aid packets. It was still three days until his routine scrub down, but the home had not been nearly this messy when he had left yesterday. He would have to check the vents.

This stuff must be coming from somewhere.

He relocked the door and went to the closet where they kept all of the cleaning equipment. The small broom and standing dustpan were in there, but he was looking for the long broom. He wanted to sweep up the big stuff and then run the vacuum.

After searching the upstairs for it without success, he made his way to the elevator to look downstairs. It was almost five. Harold would be back at his house by now, so he knew he wouldn't have to deal with that asshole's little temper tantrums. Try as he might to get along with the creep, Harold being the boss lady's brother, he never liked the guy and the feeling seemed more than mutual. Glenn knew that there was more than a general dislike for his fellow man behind the Harold's meanness; there was a hint of thinly veiled prejudice that Glenn had picked up on. He knew that Harold thought of him as a house nigger and nothing more, and that caused him to hate the man, though he hid it to keep his job. He and his wife had been having a hard time since the loading dock had downsized. He needed this job, even if wheeling around dead folks all day wasn't his idea of a noble or even enjoyable profession. If he weren't in his mid-forties he would reenlist in the army or maybe even join the fire department. But it was too late for that. Too late for a lot of things.

The elevator was worse than the lobby. The dirt was high enough to cover his ankles, like a playground sandbox.

What in the Sam Hill . . . ?

He kicked at it, half expecting to unearth tarantulas or something.

There was also the terrible, familiar stink of the dead.

Closing the door, Glenn hit the button, and, as he began his descent, more dust drizzled down from the top of the elevator. It filled his hair and fought its way into his eyes.

"Damn it!" he said, batting it away.

He was still rubbing it from his eyes when he made it to the basement. He slung the freight elevator's metal door open and the foul odor hit his nose like a wrecking ball. His eyes burned and blurred from it, but at least the tears pushed the remaining grains out. When he stopped rubbing them, he looked up, and even through the blur he could see that there was something pinned up on the rear wall. He wiped at his eyes with his shirtsleeves, his breath locking in his chest.

Glenn stumbled backward, stammering the gibberish of absolute fear.

The thing on the wall was an atrocity; a hideous horror the likes of which Glenn could never even conceive. It wasn't pinned to the wall; it was hovering before it like a shrine unto itself. All around this thing, a swarm of red lights buzzed and flew. The creature was deformed and covered in fresh stitches that oozed pink slime from its numerous limbs, making it resemble a human squid. Its tentacles, like hooked worms, didn't just squirm, they were thrashing.

It knew he was there.

The head of the beast opened its mouth and little red lights came pouring out like a fountain. He heard them buzzing now. It was a deafening thrum, causing him to clasp his hands to his ears.

They're bugs, he realized. *Thousands of red fireflies.*

As they spilled across the creature's swollen belly, he saw it bloat further, pulsing with a scarlet glow, and the stitches around the vagina tore. Between the groin and the bellybutton, the slit opened and another, different head came pushing through. Even though the eyes had been scooped out of it, he recognized it.

It was Harold, smiling at him for the first time.

Having run upstairs in a panic, Glenn pulled on the front door handle so hard that he nearly popped his arm out of its socket. He'd forgotten it was locked. The red dirt was spinning around him now, making little dust devils as the flies that had followed him up climbed his legs and neck. He got the door open, but a mighty gust started to blow it shut again, and he had to put both hands in the wedge to try and force it open. Even with all his strength pulling it, the door started slamming on his fingers, but he held tight and kept pulling. With one hard thrust, he got it mostly open and managed to slide it half way out. The door pressed against him like a vise, but he had just enough leverage to squeeze himself through if he sucked in his gut.

He popped out of the jamb and ran into the darkness of the pre-dawn morning. He ran hard and fast, faster than he had since he was in his twenties. He didn't even feel the normal, arthritic pain in the knee he had shattered years back. All he felt was the terror. It was pounding in his mind and making him rush like he'd been given a heavy adrenaline shot. The quivering fear was relentless. It kept him running, kept him shaking, kept him screaming all the way down the street, passing his car, passing every porch light and open business. He just wanted to run—run forever—and never, ever come back.

Chapter Thirty

Javier loaded up the bagged body and got into the driver's seat.

He was returning it. Not because he cared if Harold needed it, but because Javier didn't want to be bothered with the disposal. Besides, he wanted to see what other juicy bits the undertaker had.

He drove into the street and took a pull on his flask. It was nearing six. The house would be looking for breakfast soon, but they could wait. He wanted to get the corpse out of the house before it started to stink any worse. It was already bad enough with the guts spilling out. That *chíca salvaje* had gone *loca*.

By seven he made it into the center of town where the funeral home was. He went around back as always and saw that Harold's car was there. The undertaker kept crazy hours, practically lived in the place. Javier trusted he would still be there, especially considering that the corpse had not been returned yet.

He got the bag out, walked around to the back door, and knocked. He waited for a while and then pulled on the knob. It was locked and he didn't want to go around front with the body, so he picked it with the locksmith tool he carried on his belt. He stepped into the black corridor and made his way into the far hall, noticing the dust all over the wall.

Jesus, this shit is everywhere. Must be something in the

wind. A sand storm pushing through like the ones he'd dealt with growing up in shit-ass Guerrero seemed like a stretch. *Maybe it was something blowing down from the distant mountains*, he thought, *from piles of molded leaves or some sort of pollen.*

He got into the elevator, snarling from the pungent stench, and went down to the basement. He slid open the door and, before he could even step inside, he saw it. He dropped the bag and stood there in awe.

¡Dios mío!

The monstrosity seemed to swim in the air, stroking its limbs in every direction. It had a hot pink sheen and red bugs circled its head like a halo. Its body was clearly made of mangled remains. Someone, almost certainly Harold, had stitched and stapled them together, creating an awful sight that inflamed each of the senses. It froze Javier, not so much out of fear, but out of sheer befuddlement. The thing, while disgusting, was a whole new horror even to his jaded eyes. It was a sculpture of depravity, a perverted mannequin born from madness—a waking nightmare, but also something much, much more. Something special.

This is something the world has never seen.

Chapter Thirty-One

The fog on the lake was accentuated by the rolling storm clouds that came upon the breaking dawn. Kandi watched them as she sat on the deck, glad to be out of the house for a while. Her flight home was booked for tomorrow morning and it couldn't come fast enough.

She was more than weary.

Her mind was in pain and her soul was sick.

They had just a few dialogue scenes to shoot and then it would be a wrap. She found herself thinking maybe this would be her final shoot too, her final film—not just for this underground circuit, but for the adult industry all together. After all she'd seen in these dark mountains, she doubted that she could ever be comfortable doing a sex scene again. It would only open these fresh and terrible memories, which would dry her vagina and wet her eyes.

She thought about Dr. Wong, the therapist she and David had seen when things fell apart, and whom she had continued to see for a while after David left. She thought now would be a good time to reconnect with her, but she didn't know how to begin telling her what she'd seen, what she'd *done*, patient confidentiality or not.

The water of the lake was cool and therapeutic on her sore feet. It seemed as if every inch of her body ached, as if punishing her. She lit a cigarette, her first one in years, and took another pull on the bottle of vodka she had taken from the bar. She hoped it would bring her down enough to get her to sleep. She'd been up all night, unable to get comfortable in the bed, as well as in her thoughts. She wanted the booze to black her out now, and she didn't care about the hangover or vomiting that might come with it. Escape was needed, and she wanted to fall into alcohol's numbing web and let it wrap her up so that the big, black spider of drunkenness could eat her alive.

It began to drizzle and it felt good, washing away the bits of red dust that had accumulated just since her shower. It reminded her of a time, so long ago, when she was innocent and pure. A time that, while fleeting, had been much happier than she realized it was when she was living it. Kandi knew she could never go back, but she hoped that perhaps there was some sort of medium between that innocent time and the dank, seemingly bottomless pit she had sank into after David had gone, which had eventually led her back into the industry, and then into this simmering, red-dusted hell of hate-fucking and blood.

Maybe there could be a new, different job. Maybe even a new man; one that would treat her at least half as good as David had, which might be more than she deserved. She wondered if it was possible. She wondered if whatever forces controlled this world would allow her such a luxury after what she'd done.

Thunder shook the walls and Toby's eyes snapped open. He had fallen asleep, but he was not sure for how long. He remembered the Mexican coming in and trying to feed him a tuna fish sandwich, which Toby had refused even though he was very hungry, but that was the last thing he could remember. It could have been hours ago or a day ago.

The lights were off and only a sliver of grey, morning light could knife through the curtains, giving the room soft shadows. He still had to pee, but he didn't bother to call out for somebody. He almost felt afraid to, as if the Mexican would make some sadistic game out of it and laugh at him while he punched Toby's gut until he pissed his pants.

How much longer am I going to be here?

His body ached from the hard chair. His ass was as numb as his wrist, and his back made him feel like a tractor-sized linebacker had sacked him. Stomach gurgling, he hoped that a shit wasn't coming on too.

As if his thoughts had transmitted telepathically, the door opened and in stepped Rutger. His face was haggard and held the same dull grey as the room. He closed the door behind him.

"How you doing kid?" he asked.

How the fuck do you think I'm doing, old man?

"I need to use the bathroom," he said.

"That can be arranged. I'm sure you'd like to stretch your legs too. But I'll tell you now that you'll have to go right back into the chair afterward, until we finish wrapping this thing up. It won't be long now though, thank God."

Rutger had a different demeanor about him than before. There was no cocky stride or shyster smile.

"I'm sorry about this, kid," he said. "About all of it. Sometimes things don't go as planned in life. Things slip away from you and then you slip away from yourself. I never thought I'd end up here. I'm sure you're thinking the same thing about yourself, and about Jessica."

"You've got that right."

Rutger stepped closer and put his hands on Toby's shoulders.

"Your girlfriend wants to stay involved in this. I don't just mean porn; I mean dark street porn. The kind of stuff you have to know somebody to get your hands on, somebody bad.

"Few professions have the fatality rate of ours. Jessica's young and misguided. I think she's even mentally ill in some way. Once this movie is over, and it will be today, I assure you, I'd like to ask you to do whatever it takes to get her out of here as soon as possible. I'm going to give her a fake name in the film and no one who knows her will ever see it. Even she won't. I won't give my employers her real name either. They'll want her for more, I can assure you, but I'll tell them everything she gave me was false information. She will want to come back here, Toby. She will want to be a part of all of this. But I'm getting out, and I don't think I'll be staying here very long. I want to find a new home for a new start."

Toby felt a small nugget of hope. He clutched it tight.

We're going to get out of this okay.

"Get her some help, son," Rutger said. "It's not too late to save her. She can get a new start too. If you love her the way I think you do, you'll take her to her mama, then a doctor or her priest or whatever; just some kind of support group. Get her on some meds, maybe."

"I will," Toby said. "I really will. But right now I just want to get us as far away from here as possible, for good."

"Well, kid, I've gotta tell ya, that's exactly where the two of you belong."

Chapter Thirty-Two

The rain was loud upon the roof and the jeep splashed through the puddles that were forming in the dips, making wave sounds as it wound through the mountain's muddy trails.

In the back, The Goddess lay still—waiting, anticipating, and gleaming from within the zipped body bag. It was too tight for her many limbs, but The Goddess knew no pain or discomfort now. She knew only the bliss of decay and the sweetness of her suffocating, black desires that spread through her heart like mildew. Pink pus oozed from pores and she marinated in her own delectable filth. She would lay dormant now, until the time was nigh. She was preparing her flesh for what she somehow knew was the next step, however nebulous it may be. She had sensed the driver's potent evil even before Harold had been able to murmur his identity and seedy background to The Goddess from the rotted core of her heavy womb.

The flies, her death spawn, cooked gory musings in her organs. She could taste their second-long thoughts and the harmony of their pending frenzy echoed in her head, making her harshly attached face slide on the slickness of her skull.

Harold quivered too. She could feel his head undulating and his shrunken body shaking beneath it as he wiggled like an excited child within her. Her sweet lover had become one with her, sharing the same morbid passions and connecting their mutual blood dreams. The two of them churned as a single entity, spinning slowly in the bag, his touch from within her making her flush toward an orgasm. His baby hands stroked her inner walls and his half-inch erection rubbed at her internal clitoris. The feeling was electric—just as charged as the thunderstorm that brewed outside in an ominous welcome to the world beyond the basement that lay in wait for her touch.

Chapter Thirty-Three

Kandi turned around when she heard the car reach the house. She was still on the deck letting the rain cleanse her. She watched Javier get out and take something long and black from the back. At first she thought it was some kind of inner tube, but when she saw how he had to brace it over his shoulder to pick it up, and how it fell slack over him, she knew better.

No, please. Not another body.

But she knew it could be nothing else. She could only hope she wouldn't have to look at it, considering the ghastly shape the last one had been in even before Jessica had torn it open and Billy had goddamned fucked its guts. One thing she knew for certain was that she wouldn't have anything to do with it. She wouldn't even allow for it to be propped up next to her in a dialogue sequence. The bloodlust had a way of taking over. She didn't trust herself to be capable of fighting it off anymore. Worse still, there was Jessica, and who knew what that sick bitch would do.

Javier carried the bag in and placed it before the steps that went down into the living room. *It must be heavy,* Rutger thought, because Javier was breathing hard like a panting dog.

Billy was sitting across from him. He'd had a glazed look in his eye as they drank scotch together in near silence, but now Billy seemed to come back from the retreat of his mind. He looked at the printing on the leather bag on the floor.

"Property of Ruben Funeral Home," Billy said. "Aw, fuck."

Javier smiled like a jack-o-lantern, only spookier.

"And just what is this?" Rutger asked.

"Just wait until you see," Javier told him.

"I'm not so sure I want to."

"Oh, you do. You really do."

"I'm serious, Javier. I don't want any more dead bodies in here. The shoot is over."

"Mr. Malone," he said. "Listen to me. This is different. This could be a *million dollar finale.*"

Rutger sighed and looked down into the thin swirl of his remaining drink. He knew that he would need another. It was almost morning now, but what the hell? He hadn't slept. He doubted anyone had.

"But we're done," he said. "We had a finale that's just as fucked up as can be and—"

"No," Javier said. He pointed to the bag at his feet. "What's in here is so fucked up it makes everything we've done so far look like child's play. You always say you want to make art of bodies, right?"

Rutger nodded, breath escaping him, deflating his shoulders.

"Well," Javier said, unzipping the bag. "Somebody else had the same idea."

Kandi didn't see Jessica until she was already past the back porch's screen. She'd walked back toward the pool, and the sudden movement of the girl coming out of the water made Kandi's heart leap as well as her feet.

Jessica looked at her in puzzlement. "Are you okay?"

"You just startled me."

"Yeah. Seems like I'm scaring everyone lately."

It was still raining steadily and something about Jessica having been swimming in it seemed strange and unnatural. The girl looked extra pale against the backdrop of the rippling blue water and her freckles were extra bright in the budding dawn, like tiny cherries bleeding out of her skin. Kandi could swear there were twice as many on her than there had been before.

"It's just that I'm not feeling all that well," Kandi said. "Too much drink I suppose."

But that wasn't it.

Try as she might, the drunkenness she craved just wouldn't come. She'd emptied the bottle and still wasn't even walking funny. At least, not that she noticed.

"I'll bet you're glad to be going home tomorrow," Jessica said.

"Yes. I miss L.A. I miss my house and my things. I'll be glad to be home again. Won't you?"

Jessica began to float on her back, letting the rain fall upon her front.

Are her breasts bigger?

"There's nothing for me . . . back home. Nothing."

"That's not true. You have Toby for one thing."

"Toby's leaving. Everything that's good does. You know that."

"What do you mean?"

"You know how all good things leave, Kandi. Like your innocence, your youth, and your husband, David."

Kandi locked up hearing Jessica say his name. She hadn't told her anything personal, especially not anything about

David. The only person who could have told her anything about him would have to be Rutger, but why would he?

"How do you know about my husband?" she asked.

"You told me."

"I *didn't.*"

"He's written all over you, Kandi. It's in the sad, purple sheen under your eyes and in the downward curve of the sides of your mouth. Your whole body aches for him. I could smell that ache on you when we fucked."

She's crazy. I knew she was fucked in the head, but she's even worse than I imagined. She's a downright psycho.

"You don't know anything about my pain," Kandi said.

"Oh, but I do. I know *everyone's* pain. Rutger's remorse over never having a child; Javier's regret over abandoning his sick mother and younger siblings to run from the Mexican police; Billy's secret longing for other men that he just can't face. I know all of it. Their pain spills out to me. That's why they want to fuck me so hard and see me fucked so hard. All men do, and so do most women. They want to see me crushed and cripple me with fuck, to let their pain squirt out of their bodies so my pussy, ass, and mouth can swallow it up for them, so I can process their miseries into something more important."

"And just what is that?" Kandi asked, mad at the sick bitch now.

"Into art, of course. Into art."

The body was more than one body. It was several parts of several women all fused together into a gruesome edifice. It was a mélange of flesh—a downright hellish puzzle sown together by a tortured mind. Rutger put down his drink. It wouldn't help him anymore. Not now.

"Who the hell did this?" he asked, staring.

"It must have been the undertaker," Javier said. "I think some of these pieces came from that torso we had in here earlier. Incredible isn't it?"

"Incredible? It's a fucking *abomination*."

Javier laughed, raspy from years of smoking cigars.

Billy stood up and walked out of the room without a word. A few seconds later they heard a door slam shut behind him.

"What's up his ass?" Javier asked.

Rutger wiped his brow and sighed, his head hung deep into his chest. There was a dull, hopeless sorrow in him now. He wanted to fly to some far away place, maybe Rome or Paris, where no one knew him so he could pretend he was indeed someone new, and forget about the man he'd become for a while. He wanted to get a hotel room with a spectacular view and eat exotic meals that would fill his belly and woo him into thirteen hours of sleep a night.

That's all he wanted. *Was that too much to ask?*

He wanted to kick Javier in the teeth for bringing this ghastly grotesque into his manor. They were going to film the connective dialogue sequences. That was it and that was all. No more bodies. No more eviscerations. No more atrocities. Javier knew this, and yet the bastard had hauled this *thing* into the house and wanted to use it in his picture. It was insulting. It was downright rude.

"Take it back to the undertaker, Javier. I don't want it in my house."

Javier stood up and looked at him as if heartbroken.

"You can't be serious. This here is beautiful." His yellow teeth shined. "*Una gran obra*."

"I understand that I've asked you for horrible things like this in the past and I'll admit that—sweet Jesus—you've outdone yourself this time, but the picture is finished and so am I. Bring this . . . this . . . fucking . . . *creature* to Vic if you want to see it in a movie so bad."

Now it was Javier who got angry. He stepped in closer.

"I don't want it in some cheap splatter movie," he said. "It deserves better than that. It's too *magnífico*, too lovely. It deserves to be in one of *your* movies. *This* movie."

"I'm sorry, Javier but . . . "

"Sorry? You're *sorry*? Nah, that ain't good enough. You think I'm just here to make you dinner and do your dirty work? You think I'm just your pissant servant? Have you forgotten who I really work for? I'm here to make sure that you have everything you need to deliver a quality product to the organization. I'm here to make sure that you make the best movie possible."

Rutger was taken aback. Javier was imposing and demonstrating his power to him for the first time. It was not a development he had anticipated and it made him rethink just what his relationship with Vic really boiled down to.

"You *will* put this creature into the movie," Javier said. "You'll do it one way or another. You don't have to like it. None of your people do. No one has to like it except for the organization, and the hundreds of thousands of customers we serve."

Javier continued to step in and now Rutger could smell the man's breath. It was foul, reeking of alcohol and death. There was a cruelty in his eyes that was harder than he had ever seen. His professional courtesy was gone.

The servant had become the master.

The crew returned at six that afternoon, as planned, and began setting up in the living room. They expected to shoot a dialogue sequence on the couch, then a few sexless bedroom scenes, and finally a nude pool scene where the women would swim together but not lead into anything more interesting than that.

Ben was his usual jovial self, but Tye and Mia still held

the sour look they'd had when they'd left the previous night. The fluffer had not come back at all. There was a bitterness to them all now that was palpable, and they kept their distance from Kandi, Billy, and Rutger.

Kandi hadn't seen Jessica since the pool that morning and she was glad for it. The girl had gone from creepy to maniacal. Her words had stung Kandi and lingered like a gypsy curse. She didn't know where Jessica was now and frankly she didn't want to. She just wanted her to get in front of the camera on time, shoot the simple scenes, and then leave her alone for the rest of the night so she could fly home tomorrow and never have to talk to her again.

At first she had pitied the girl. She had tried to talk her out of making all the mistakes she had made over the past few days. But now she could see that Jessica was sick and hopeless. There was an evil inside of her, just like there was in this house, and Kandi wanted away from them both.

Rutger was pacing, not in a creative brainstorm, but as if in a nervous dilemma. She figured he was probably as broken down now as she was. In spite of all that he'd done in the name of these films, Kandi felt that he was a good man at heart. He had never wanted to hurt anybody unless they wanted to be hurt. He didn't do pedophile porn, torture films, or rape movies. He was a purveyor of only consensual blood baths and that said a lot about a man in the world of underground, illegal porn.

Billy was sitting next to her on the couch. He looked like a zombie, a brainwashed cult member or victim of a memory-erasure like in a sci-fi movie.

He probably didn't get any more sleep than I did. Jesus, how the hell could he?

The only one who seemed okay was Jessica. She didn't seem rested, but appeared tireless and unbothered by what she had done. The girl was impossible to rattle it seemed. She was impervious to the mental and emotional strain caused by these despicable acts, as if humanity held no value, if it had ever existed in the first place.

Just as Kandi was thinking of her, Jessica came out of her room, as if summoned by some unspoken song. She, like Kandi, was dressed in a skin-hugging cocktail dress—Kandi's powder blue to compliment her blonde hair and creamy skin, Jessica's pale green to accentuate her red hair and emerald eyes. She stepped into the living room, and when she sat across from them, neither Kandi nor Billy kept her gaze.

"Ready for the boring parts?" Jessica asked.

Neither of them replied.

"That's all right," Jessica said. "That's just fine."

Kandi couldn't tell if she was being snarky or genuinely resigned.

Ben waddled over and tried to strike up a conversation, seeing as the rest of the crew was in a nasty mood.

"The hard stuff is over," he said. "You guys did a great job."

"Thank you," Jessica said.

Kandi noticed that even Ben was keeping a safe distance. He stood next to where Kandi sat, a little bit behind the sofa even.

"This shouldn't take but an hour or two," he said. "Personally, I don't see the point of these sequences, given the nature of the movie. People don't care about the plot even in straight porn. There's no way the splatter crowd will give a damn."

"You think that because you're a fool," Jessica said. "You don't know art from a cartoon show, fat shit. That's why you're a cameraman and not a filmmaker."

Ben stood there for a moment, speechless. Kandi hoped he wouldn't dignify the girl's viciousness with a comeback. She wanted things to be as smooth as they could be today so nothing could slow production.

"No need to get all personal," Ben said, quietly. "It was just my opinion."

Kandi looked up at Jessica. Her eyes were wide and her face looked different somehow. Her chin seemed bigger and her forehead seemed longer. Beneath her dress her tits were swollen and impossibly huge. She couldn't be sure, but she thought she could see something in her eyes too, as if small, red worms were swimming in her pupils. She tried to tell herself it was just the lighting.

Ben walked off before Jessica could say another nasty word. Kandi felt like shaking herself loose, so she got up and went to the bar and poured herself a shot. She was just about to knock it back when she saw that Jessica had stood up and now was watching her.

"Oh, Kandi," Jessica said. "What would David say if he could see you now?"

Chapter Thirty-Four

With the sharpest of the tools splayed out on the coffee table, they were just about to begin when Javier brought it out into the higher section of the living room where the imported love seats surrounded fireplace. He stretched out the bag on the carpet and began to unzip it. Before he could get it all the way open and unwrap the beast within, Kandi turned to Rutger with a pinched face.

"What the fuck is this?" she whispered. "We're doing quick dialogue scenes. That's all. No more of this horrible fucking shit, you understand me?"

"Look," he said. "I don't like this either, Kandi. But it has to be done."

"What? What has to be done?"

"One final scene . . . with a body."

"No!"

Javier turned his head for a moment but then went back to lifting the carcass's upper half out of the bag.

"Please, keep your voice down," Rutger said. "Javier is running the show now. You don't want him to hear you objecting to this."

"I thought he worked for you."

"I had come to believe that too, but I was foolish to think so. He works for Vic, and Vic says the sicker a picture is the better it sells, and what's in that bag is definitely sick."

"Wasn't gutting a torso like a fish enough for these perverts?"

Before he could answer Tye yelled, "Oh, hell no!"

Javier had the bag open and Tye was walking around the room aimlessly, his arms going up and down in the air in a tantrum.

"This is it, man!" Tye said. "This is the motherfuckin' line."

Javier went over to Tye and blocked his path.

Rutger didn't like where this was going.

"Oh my God," Kandi said, seeing the grotesque thing on the floor.

"You've filmed plenty of dead bodies before," Javier said to Tye. "Why is this suddenly a problem?"

"*What's the problem?* Look at the fuckin' thing, man!"

Mia had been in the bathroom. She came out of the hall just as Tye was pointing down at the body. She took one look at it, covered her mouth, and went running back the way she had come, but Javier put an arm out in front of her.

"Listen to me," he said. "*All of you*!"

His voice was calm but commanding.

"We are going to film one more sex scene," Javier said. "With this body."

Jessica stood up now, curious for a look. She made her way forward and stared down at it, speechless, and didn't move or even breathe.

"I'm not filming *shit*," Tye said. "I'm done. I get paid by the day. You can keep the goddamned money, I'm out!"

"You're not out," Javier said. "Nobody is out."

"It's so beautiful," Jessica said, but Rutger doubted the arguing men had heard her.

Billy and Ben were both watching the situation spin out of control. They looked as uncomfortable as Rutger felt.

Kandi's hand wrapped around his arm and squeezed as the room hummed with quiet tension.

"Just film it, Tye," Rutger said. "Please."

"Fuck you, Rutger!" he said. "I'm done making movies with your sick ass. Five years in film school just to end up making this bullshit. I should have stuck to filming that NASCAR shit for all them dumbass hillbillies."

"Please," Rutger said, hoping Tye would realize it was for his own good.

"You should listen to your director," Javier said.

There was a growl to his voice now, low but noticeable. He got closer to Tye; dangerously close. Mia whimpered his name in soft plea.

Tye didn't budge. "He's not my director, *asshole*!"

Javier slugged Tye in the chest and he crumbled. But Tye was young and strong and, still in a crouch, he sent a fist into Javier's stomach. Javier bent from the impact and Tye came in with the uppercut. Rutger had forgotten about Tye's passion for kickboxing. Javier was outmatched. Tye was up on his feet while Javier was still wobbling, and he took advantage of this and spun, attempting to roundhouse kick Javier into the wall. Rutger tensed with hope now; hope that Javier would be knocked unconscious and that they could sink this weird body in the lake and call everything quits.

But Javier saw the kick coming and managed to dodge it, and it was all the time he needed to reach for the pistol he kept tucked into the back of his jeans. In that instant, Rutger wished that he or Billy or even Ben had helped Tye while they'd had the chance by grabbing Javier from behind. But everything happened so fast, just like the gunshot.

The top of Tye's head came off in a wet chunk.

It splattered the brickwork with blood, brains, and fragments of skull.

Thunder moaned.

Tye fell backward with his arms flailing as the sound of the shot made everyone cover their ears just a little too late.

Rutger's ears began to ring and he couldn't hear what Javier was yelling anymore. He was cursing at Tye's body, as if he was trying to provoke him back from the dead for another duel. Even though he could not hear them, Rutger knew that Kandi and Mia were screaming. Ben was hiding behind his camera as if he was next on Javier's hit list, and Billy remained paralyzed by what he'd seen.

The ringing began to fade and the shock of what had just happened began to sink in. Even though Rutger was sweating, he felt cold suddenly, the summer breeze coming through from the porch felt like an arctic blast. He watched Javier raise his pistol straight up with his arm bent at the elbow. The man's black eyes scanned the room like a viper.

"Anyone else have any objections?" Javier asked.

No one did.

They were going to film the scene.

Rutger watched Tye's head leak onto the floor and spread about in a sticky pool. Jessica had knelt down to get a better look at the multi-armed corpse and the blood was now pooling around her feet and knees. She didn't seem to notice it. She was too busy running her hands all over the weird body to even notice Tye's. She seemed enticed by it, perhaps aroused by it even; spellbound.

Rutger took over Tye's camera and Javier sat in the director's seat next to him. It was time for his ideas to be heard; Billy knew that now. Kandi was laying on the long couch as instructed while Jessica sat in the loveseat in front of the corpse. No one had moved or cleaned up Tye.

Tye was a star now.

Billy was kneeling before the strange corpse, trying desperately to jerk himself erect enough to fuck this horrible thing the way Javier had told him to. But he was too afraid.

He could feel Javier's murderous eyes burning into his back like cinders. The fear of his failure to perform was making it a reality and he was starting to shake. He didn't want to end up like Tye. He'd rather hump this pile of body parts than have his head cracked like a dropped watermelon. But he didn't know if he could. Not alone.

"Mr. Javier," he said. "Do you think one of the girls could help me out here?"

He saw Kandi grimace.

Fuck you, lady. How do you think I feel?

Before Javier could reply Jessica slid off the loveseat and began to crawl toward Billy like a tiger. Her smile was twisted and weird, like her lips were being sucked back into her mouth. Billy thought he could hear a buzzing coming off of her, but his ears were still ringing a little from the shot. When she reached him, she climbed over the corpse and lied down upon it, making the gas of the dead escape from all of the places it was stitched. Billy almost felt like he would pass out, but Jessica seemed to enjoy it. She breathed in deep as if it was a blooming flower garden.

She cupped his balls and starting blowing him. He was still shaking, but he closed his eyes and tried to concentrate on her tongue dancing along the bottom of his limp cock. He felt it stirring now. Jessica was good at fellatio, so there was a chance she could get him to stand at attention despite the circumstances. He knew he would only be happy about that until it was time to stick it to the cold corpse—to pump the grey vagina that had obviously been ripped out of one body and stapled into this one.

Billy thought of Derek, the grocery stocker at Whole Foods who had been his secret crush for months. He tried to imagine that it was Derek's mouth on him now instead of Jessica's. Her mouth was very warm, hot even, as if she had just filled her mouth with cinnamon tea. Her tongue made waves beneath him, around him, slurping him up. Her pink muscle seemed to do the impossible. It shrouded his shaft entirely, like a pig in a blanket, and began milking him. Had it not been for his nervousness, he would have cum immediately. This was good, he thought. He was rock hard and ready to pop. He could give it to the corpse for a few thrusts and then pop out and spray it. Done deal.

Billy exited Jessica's mouth and spit in his hand to open the corpse's vagina. But he found that it was already wet. More than that, it was warm, impossibly warm, and it was throbbing as if anticipating him. He stepped away.

"That thing is warm!" Billy said. "Its fucking pussy is wet! What the fuck is this thing?"

Jessica was sitting on the corpse's face now, grinding.

"She isn't a thing, Billy," Jessica said. "She's a goddess and she deserves our worship."

Jessica could feel The Goddess's tongue climbing into her vagina like a serpent. It must have been a foot long and as thick as a beer bottle. It rolled inside Jessica's inner walls, pissing its tongue-goo from its tip. She felt it spatter within her and stick to the deepest part of her womanhood like a huge wad of semen. She shuddered with delight and fell back onto The Goddess, lapping at her stitches and letting her pink ooze drool upon her cheeks.

In her belly, the babies began to spin.

Kandi wanted to run.

If she took off her high heels she might just make it to the door before Javier could draw the gun from the back of his jeans. But she knew the gates would be locked. She looked to the rest of the group. Rutger and Ben were hidden behind their cameras and Javier was stoic in his seat, cracking his knuckles as he watched. Billy was ghostly pale. He looked on the verge of tears.

It was strange.

There was no bloodlust in the air, not for her and obviously not for Billy. The only one who seemed to feel it this time was Jessica, as if she had gotten all of it for herself. She writhed on the corpse, wrapping its limp arms around her and snaking its legs through her arms and shoulders. She was sixty-nine-ing it, and from where Kandi was sitting, she could see Jessica's ass moving back and forth upon its head.

But that's not what bothered her.

What bothered her were the quick glimpses of Jessica's vagina on the corpse's mouth whenever she thrust forward.

The corpse's tongue was moving.

Jessica made a sound that wasn't even human and Billy stumbled backward. It was a noise like a cat makes when in heat, only louder and more ferocious. It was nearly as loud as the gunshot had been and Billy once again put his hands to his ears.

The upshot was that nobody cared what he was doing anymore. All eyes were on the crazy bitch that was having a wild oral session with the one she kept calling The Goddess.

"Rise, my Goddess," she said in the brief moments she came up for air. "Rise."

Billy wasn't sure what Jessica wanted to rise.

He just knew it wouldn't be him anymore.

The thunder began to shake the whole house as the world outside grew blacker. When the lights flickered, the room didn't go black, it went pink. At first Rutger thought it was something in the camera, but when he pulled his eye away and looked around he could see that bright redness was spreading up and out of the corpse like it was a pile of simmering coals.

A boom ruptured the heavens and the lights went out entirely and the house became a scarlet cathedral. The high ceiling filled with shadows and Jessica's psychotic roaring was accompanied by a horrible buzzing noise. The house thrummed, ignited.

Rutger looked at Jessica. She had pulled the top of her dress down and the skirt part up, so it looked like she had on only a thick belt. Her breasts were huge now, D-cups at least, and they were firm and perfectly round. Her freckles had not only multiplied, they were continuing to multiply, spreading like a rash, changing amounts so quickly that it was noticeable to the naked eye even in the red illumination. But the light wasn't dim, not at all. It was if they were inside a neon light. Everything was tinted red, but it was all clear as crystal.

He thought about the red dust that had been filling the house and how it seemed to multiply with each shoot they did. He knew now that the sandy redness was coming to them more with each atrocity they created, like hornets being drawn to a nest, helping it grow bigger and stronger, gaining strength from their wickedness while also throwing gas on its fire.

Kandi was right. There was an evil entity here and they had been feeding it, and now he feared that it had grown so big that it needed even more to satiate its appetite. It wanted an atrocity to match itself, he thought, like a sadomasochistic marriage of horror, and it was finding it now in Jessica's embrace.

"I want cock!" Jessica screamed.

Billy covered his crotch with both hands.

She was foaming.

She could feel her spittle spilling down her chin. Her whole face was glazed by The Goddess's moist hole, christened by her juices. Now Jessica wanted to be fucked and for The Goddess to get the fucking she rightly deserved as well, so she slid off and began her kitten crawl toward Billy again.

She hoped that Javier would stick the gun right into Billy's stupid, goddamned mouth. The little queer was being a wimp. He was here to provide one thing: a stiff dick. Most men would kill for the chance to screw her and Kandi, and here he was shaking like a Chihuahua in the rain. It sickened her.

Jessica reached out for him, but Billy bounced back again, this time hitting the wall. She pounced up and the lightning cracked outside, filling the room with white flashes. The thunder boomed in the walls and shook the chandelier, and as it did she heard a sound like a freight train coming from behind her.

The Goddess sat up and her mouth was open, her jaw unhinged. She was breathing out a cyclone of the red dust. It blew all about, making the room even redder. Everyone else covered their eyes. The dust slipped into every fold and filled every crack. It clung to the ceiling as well as the walls and ground into them, scratching loudly like scurrying cockroaches.

Jessica watched The Goddess rise up, her arms and legs swimming in the air, supported by the power of the dust. The Goddess levitated, and as she did the pink goo began to pour out of her vagina and ass. It splashed across the floor like a big blob of Pepto-Bismol, covering Tye's body and splashing everyone's legs. Inside of the slime were what looked like pumpkin seeds.

Jessica reached into the goo and pulled one out. The shell was soft and yielding.

It's an egg.

When she looked up again, The Goddess had reached the ceiling and was beginning to lay its back against it. The slime was mixing with the dust now and creating a grainy sort of blood syrup. The wind continued, but the dust was sticking. The others began to open their eyes so they too could see the splendor of this heavenly creature.

Jessica watched on, tearing up from the emotions that flooded her. She saw The Goddess's jaw snap into place and the dead eyes opened wide as her stomach began to balloon and glow. The skin of the creature's belly stretched taut, something rolling beneath it, making the flesh flex and struggle. The stitched part between the vagina and the abdomen stretched and the stitches started to snap from the pressure. A black dot appeared from within and then began growing, making a dark oval in The Goddess's lower body. Her arms and legs moved like they were being manipulated by an unseen puppeteer, and from out of the opening, a man's head emerged. It was slick with blood and his hair was knotted with fireflies.

He scanned the room smiling, even though he had no eyes.

Chapter Thirty-Five

Evil. It was all about them, all around them. Kandi screamed.

She was no longer concerned about Javier's gun. She got up and ran to the door, but the slime had covered the handle, and when she tried to turn it, she could get no traction. Her hands just slid and slid in the oiliness.

Looking back into the room, Kandi saw Ben heading for the open door to the porch. Mia dropped the boom and followed behind him, but Javier stood up and grabbed her by the hair. From her own momentum she spun forward, and Javier slammed her down onto her back. Ben was just about to round the pool when Javier drew his Colt and shot him in the hip, and he tripped and splashed into the water.

Javier spun back around and Kandi could see that a new darkness had fallen across the man's face. It was more than his usual, haggardly, busted appearance. Javier had the bloodlust look. But no matter how dangerous he could be, he was not nearly as disconcerting as the oozing ghoul that swam above them in its own hot-pink filth.

Javier pulled Mia up by the hair. "Go help Ben out of the

pool!" His spittle slathered her face. "Then both of you get back in here. We're not through yet!"

Mia scampered through the door and Javier kept the gun on her the whole time. Ben had made it to the pool stairs and Mia bent down, put her arms under his shoulders, and helped him out. His pelvis was gushing blood and he leaned on her to walk.

Rutger turned to Javier and grabbed the man's shirt in his fist.

"Are you insane?" he said. "Look at that thing. Look at it!"

The two men turned up their heads and Kandi looked up with them.

The creature was squirming, convulsing in mid-air, and the head that stuck out of its engorged belly began to cackle. Bugs ran in and out of the pits of its eyes as if they were ant hills.

"It's some kind of fucking *demon*," Rutger said. "Can't you see that?"

"All the more reason to capture it on camera," Javier said. "Don't you see? This is *it*, Rutger. This is your *masterpiece*."

Mia and Ben were forced back to their posts and Rutger returned to his camera too, each of them under Javier's command. Ben was ghost-white; Mia couldn't stop sobbing.

By now Jessica had Billy's cock in her hands and she was pulling on it like tug of war. She wheeled him around by it and he slipped in Tye's blood and fell spinning to the floor, so she jumped on top of him. He wasn't erect yet, but Jessica knew how to get him excited. Something was guiding her—a foreign, commanding force. She scooped up some of the pink ooze and slathered his cock with it and began to stroke. She felt his cock stiffen immediately, plumping from the intoxicating elixir. It made her pussy sop and her asshole pucker. Once he was hard enough she shoved him inside of her and began to twirl upon it as if she was hula hooping. She bucked and brayed, animal-like, fucking him in the ooze and the blood as The Goddess watched from above, raining down festoons of filth that carried more eggs within its mucus. As it poured upon her, she rubbed it over her heaving chest and down to her clitoris. Billy was huge inside of her now and as hard as a tire iron. But his face was still wide with fear. The goo had made his body betray him. She smiled at poor Billy, but he remained paralyzed by his fright.

Tye's carcass was near enough for Jessica to reach over and run her left hand in his blood. It was everywhere now. She'd never realized how much a head wound could gush. She brought her hand up to her mouth, slurped at the gore, and then went back for seconds. She lapped a few times like that, all while riding Billy, and then she reached farther, digging into Tye's brains. She used her nails to rip away a spongy fragment, held it up with two fingers, and dangled it over her mouth like she was a baby bird awaiting her mother's regurgitation. She let it fall and closed her mouth around the gelatinous bulb. It was rubbery and acidic, otherworldly in its immaculate taste, as if God's personal chef had prepared it just for her.

Javier was watching her.

His crooked grin was maniacal and diseased. His unpredictable capacity for violence had turned her on and she wanted him now, bad. Still riding Billy, she curled her finger to motion him forward. He took the hint and walked up to her, feverishly unbuckling his jeans. He plopped out his short, fat cock and grabbed the back of her head. She let her tongue glide across her lips invitingly and then took him in her mouth. He was very salty and smelled as if he hadn't bathed in a few days.

Delicious.

"Kandi!" Javier shouted. "Get your pretty ass over here."

With her face buried in Javier's pubes, Jessica heard but did not see Kandi come walking over. She heard her gasp and fall to her knees beside her. Javier must have forced her down. He passed his erection from her mouth to Kandi's and back again, slapping them with it. Jessica giggled when she realized Kandi was crying.

A moan came from overhead and they all looked up to see The Goddess. The male head in her stomach had stretched out on a long, flexible, tube-like neck and had made its way up to reach the female head upon the shoulders. They were tongue-kissing and groaning as one entity. The Goddess's arms caressed her own body and one of the legs had bent in such a way that the foot was now halfway into her vagina.

The sight of this sent a surge through Jessica. She felt engorged by it and overcome by an uncontrollable urge to create more slaughter. She pushed Kandi aside and reached for the table where the cleaver, knife, and meat hook lay in waiting.

Kandi watched Jessica grab the cleaver and her heart skipped a beat. She crab-walked away from her and curled toward the base of the fireplace, soaking in the strange slime. Javier backed away from Jessica too, seeing the monstrous look in her eyes and the way her mouth had seemed to unhinge, revealing teeth that were a little sharper and more yellow than they had been before. Poor Billy was still trapped beneath her, and Kandi watched as Jessica raised the cleaver into the air and then brought the blade down into the center of Billy's chest.

"Somebody stop her!" Kandi screamed.

But no one did.

Jessica hacked and hacked, butchering Billy as she continued to fuck him. Billy tried to push her off, but her legs had locked around him and she was freakishly powerful now, seeming to not even feel his desperate blows to her head and body. Every time Billy hit her she just laughed louder. She chopped at his flailing arms, impossibly connecting every time, and in a few seconds one of his forearms had split. It dangled off of him in a wiggling, red slab and Jessica snapped at it like a shark. Her teeth caught it and she pulled hard, tearing the sinew and removing the meat from the bone completely. Billy was screeching like an injured child.

Kandi got up and tried to run to his aid and Jessica, without turning to see her, sucker-punched her in the stomach. The impact was like being hit with a bowling ball and she collapsed onto her back gasping for air. Lying there, she saw blood spray from Billy and spatter all over Jessica in a kaleidoscopic stew. The spurts came in strong jets now, his arteries exposed and pumping. Jessica grunted and snarled with each blow, still fucking Billy while she killed him.

All around them the white seedlings began to crackle and pop. The shells broke and all the tiny flies pushed forth. Their bottoms glowed like brake lights as they floated toward Jessica, sticking to her glistening flesh, as if drawn to her wickedness and the slaughter she had caused.

The cleaver came up once more and when it came back down this time it landed on Billy's throat. His cries turned into a gargle and blood began to rise in his mouth and bubble out of his nostrils. Jessica grabbed him by the hair and hacked his neck again, decapitating him. She rode and rode, howling in orgasmic delight. She picked up his severed head and held it high above her, letting it baptize her in blood. Then she flung it to the ceiling where the flying, two-headed beast snatched it.

Kandi watched in horror as it ripped the head in half, cracking the skull like a coconut, and both of its mouths feasted on the innards.

The bugs covered Jessica, decorating her, their bodies making hers flicker from black to red. Done with Billy, she turned around and Kandi could see that Jessica's eyes had turned entirely crimson. There was no white in their corners, no pupil and no iris. There was only the weird, terrifying red. She was caked in blood and the bugs seemed to thrive on it, getting their share of the meal. Their buzzing was vociferous. It blared like an industrial factory, shaking the walls and making the floor vibrate.

"More!" Jessica said. "*More flesh!*"

Jessica was looking at her now but was still straddling Billy's body. Kandi hoped it would give her enough time. She jumped up and ran down the hall and was surprised that Jessica did not give chase. She began turning the handles but every door was now locked. She wondered if Javier had done it.

No, she thought. *Jessica did it without even touching them.*

Chapter Thirty-Six

Toby wasn't exactly sure what was happening but he could feel its intensity. It was in the air and shuddering in the floor beneath his feet. It shook him in his chair and made his handcuffs jangle like the chains of a ghost. He'd heard the shots. And even behind the door he could smell the gore and hear the screams. He saw that someone was on the other side of the door now, frantically trying to get the knob to turn. Whoever it was really wanted in. Toby had only wanted out, but now he wasn't so sure.

Flies came in from the crack at the bottom of the door, each of them emitting an incandescent glow. They climbed up the door's back, confused, like moths on a window trying to get to the sun. These few buzzed gently, but beyond the door, Toby could hear an army of them thrumming as one in a horrible cacophony, as if the house had become a giant hive. In a panic, he struggled harder against his restraints, knowing that all hell had broken loose and that he, pinned to this chair, would have to endure it.

The doorknob stopped twisting; he heard more yelling and then high heels clacking away. A woman was sobbing and he could hear Javier's muffled grunts. Out in the living room, a demonic roar boomed, making Toby jolt so hard that he knocked the chair over and fell on his side.

Javier tore Kandi's dress apart, yanked it off of her, and pushed her into the bloody mess with Jessica. Kandi came down hard on her right knee. She felt the cap shift and pain exploded through her leg.

The monster had left the ceiling and was now hovering in the air. Its slime whirled in the wind tunnel, creating a hellish mesh of flies, goo, blood and other bodily fluids. The cyclone surrounded them all, caging them as it grew thicker and thicker, making escape impossible. A dense layer of flies had hatched and covered every inch of the ceiling. Kandi shuddered in this living nightmare.

Jessica came at her with her nails clacking in the air. They were longer now, like small talons, and they were dripping crimson. Her eyes flashed and her fangs snapped. In her hand was one of the knives, and she twirled it like a small baton in her fingers.

Kandi tried to get up, but Javier kicked her in the stomach. She gagged on her own breath and crumbled into a fetal position. From the corner of her eye, she saw Rutger coming closer with the camera mounted on his shoulder. For a moment she thought he was getting a close-up, but then he lifted the camera high and sent it crashing down on the back of Javier's head. Glass and plastic exploded as Javier fell. His gun went spinning beneath the couch and before he could get up, Rutger jumped on his back and began punching him. He boxed his ears and gave him quick shots to his ribs before Javier flung back an elbow that bloodied Rutger's nose with a crunch. He stumbled, landing on the floor next to Kandi. Not knowing what else to do she simply threw her arms around him. Jessica had watched it all happen and was giggling like a child. Even her voice sounded different, younger.

Javier had bits of debris stuck in his head and small glass shards jutting out of one side of his face. Small rivulets of blood spilled from his crown of broken plastic. He picked up the camera and checked it. Kandi could see that the light was on and it was still recording. Javier turned to Ben and Mia to check on them.

"The show must go on," he said.

Javier pointed the camera at Jessica. She was just inches from Kandi and Rutger now and still playing with her knife. But with the camera turned on her, she began to glide the blade along her blood-drenched body. She teased her nipples, getting them hard, and then sliced at one of them, sinking the blade deep under the nipple's tip. She began to bleed and kept cutting, sawing until the tip came off completely. Then she popped it into her mouth like it was jellybean.

Jessica raised her free hand in front of the camera and wiggled her fingers around. Her face seemed to glaze over, looking like she was in a trance. She took the blade and pressed it against the middle of her forearm, then carved a perfect circle around the center of the arm. She made an incision going from the circle all the way up to her wrist. Her moves were slow, calculated, as if performing a morbid strip tease for the camera and the perverts who would one day watch the film. When she reached the wrist, she let the blade sink into her palm, glided it between her middle and index finger, and brought it back down the backside of her hand, past the wrist, and all the way back down to the initial circle on her forearm. The cuts were deep and the bleeding was profuse.

Kandi and Rutger watched, crying as Jessica dropped the knife and sank the nails of her good hand into the gashes of the other and started peeling away the skin in one single flap. She separated it from the gap and then started pulling it up from the circle as if she was taking off a latex glove. As she peeled the flesh away, the gleaming, slick muscle beneath began to throb. The flies thrummed. Glasses burst and all through the house mirrors, frames, and windows exploded.

Inside her head, Kandi felt something pop from the pressure and she hoped she hadn't gone permanently deaf. In her arms, she felt Rutger groan more than she heard it, and he tried to raise his neck in his half-conscious state. His nose was broken and had already begun to swell. They had nowhere they could run, so they lay there, side by side in helplessness.

Jessica got her flesh glove all the way off. It dangled before the camera in one perfect piece and then she flung it to the creature whose hands placed the strip of flesh onto one of its arms. Two of the monster's other arms came toward it and its fingers spun webs that stitched the new skin into the old, adding the fresh flesh to its hulking mass. Watching this, Jessica clutched her hands to her chest. Her mouth fell slack and her eyes brimmed with tears of joy.

Chapter Thirty-Seven

Bliss.

Flesh, blood, sinew.

Kiss, sex, orgasm.

Harold waded inside The Goddess, one with it. Her glorious, dead flesh enveloped him in its warm puss, making him feel safe and loved, like a quivering fetus bathing in a pregnant belly. The love was omnipotent. His women, his loves and crushes, all embraced him at once. Their adoration and devotion stormed him.

Before him was the freckled one.

Her red eyes looked into him, through him, and he could feel his heart luxuriate. Her mouth steamed for him and her tears sang a sweet song of a longing having at last come to an end. This redhead's blood-slick body was a beautiful bounty to behold; round breasts, a sliver naval, jutting hips and hair like a river of flame. He desired her, as did The Goddess.

She belonged with them.

Their power was the same now—one—and they were united by it, throttled in its majesty. The freckled one knew this just as surely as they did. It was a truth that did not need to be spoken. She was offering herself to them in strips of her own skin and feeding them chunks of the damned with her killing tools.

We love you. We have always loved you.

He felt his mind sprinkling and the red dust drizzled through the tears in his cheeks and the holes in his mutated skull, purer and more elating than any heroin. It had come for him just as it had come for these smut peddlers. He knew their evil deeds. He could smell their guilt in their miserable hearts. The dust fed off of it, off of them. It sprouted anew in the blood they spilled and the humanity they sacrificed in the name of their art. It poured from his exposed sockets and sluiced through the gaps in his teeth, offering it completely to the freckled beauty, just as Harold and The Goddess did.

We have always loved you, Jessica.

As the dust came out, he saw that it was turning orange. Each grain sparked as it sank into the churning mess. The mélange swallowed the dust and ignited, making a surge of fire that encased the room and ate the furniture and the walls. The blood on the floor began to boil and steam.

Harold could see the sweat beading on his new lover's skin. He could see the freckles blooming and smelled the moisture of her mouth and pussy. He wanted to gnaw her body and pummel her guts with his love.

Inside The Goddess, just the right part of his shrunken body began to grow again, forcing its way out of The Goddess's vagina, fucking her backwards, his cock being shat out of the hollow of her womb.

Chapter Thirty-Eight

Javier had a revelation.

The scene had so much; blood, madness, and a marauding ghoul that had turned the house into its own private circle of hell. They had violence. They even had murder. They had severed limbs, self-mutilation, and cowering victims. Fire was burning and ooze was spinning. Unbridled evil had come in the form of a reanimated corpse that vomited flies.

But still he wanted more.

They needed one more element.

Innocence, he thought. *We need innocence.*

"Let me go!" Toby screamed.

He was still tied to the chair as Javier dragged him out into the hallway.

Toby gasped at the metallic smell of blood in the air and the eerie red light that had filled the house. As he was shoved into the living room, warm goo dripped upon his head and chest. It was everywhere.

Javier spun him around and Toby saw the horrible, horrible thing.

Its arms thrashed, its legs danced, and its two heads *drifted*. The dead skin flaked and the grey vagina belched, a red dick protruding from its hole.

This can't be real, Toby thought. *They've drugged me. They must have. My mind is scrambled. This cannot be reality. It can't be.*

Toby looked around him at the horrors. He saw the remaining crew shaking but still recording. Ben was bleeding and Mia had a stream of dried vomit down the front of her blouse. Tye was on the floor, his head was destroyed. On the other end of the room, Billy lay headless and mutilated. Rutger was on the floor too, cradled in Kandi's arms. The look of foul terror on her face made Toby freeze. Looking at his girlfriend, he understood why.

Jessica was a nightmare of gore.

One of her hands had been skinned and her entire body was covered with blood. Flies spun around her in worship and red dust was gathering at her feet. She stood as if hypnotized, staring up at the hovering creature. She approached it slowly, running her hands along its dangling legs and poking her fingers in and out of the stitched cuts as tenderly as a probing lover. She kissed the head of the monster's cock and then rimmed the vagina around it with her tongue.

"Jessica!" he yelled.

She turned and the monster retreated.

When Toby saw her face he began to cry.

The floating thing was not the only monster in the room.

Like an offering, Javier placed Toby directly in front of Jessica.

She remembered this body and flesh.

She had dined on its wanton sex.

This body had made her cum.

She was drawn to it, beguiled by it, and suddenly she was choked by a raging hunger.

"*You are mine,*" she said, hearing the static-filled, insect buzz of her own voice.

Toby screamed and her remaining nipple stiffened.

Jessica took the goo, knowing it could mold the reluctant flesh, undid his jeans, and covered his penis with it. His fear was insignificant. The goo was too powerful, as was Jessica. She bent down and rubbed his cock between her breasts and it grew tall and strong. With her other hand, she sent some of the goo up her ass on a single finger to lubricate her awaiting colon. She turned around then and sat on his erection. It filled her ass and she began to pump.

The Goddess watched.

Everyone watched.

Jessica fucked harder and with each thrust the flies clicked, the ooze cracked the walls and the fire coiled and lapped. The heat was pulverizing. She started to cum and the lion's roar that came from her mouth was not her own. There was another presence, a beast within. She had felt it growing inside of her, but now it was alive and howling. She was roaring, but the presence was roaring behind her roar.

She was its vessel.

She was *the doorway*.

Her ass was so sensitive now that she could feel the exact moment that Toby would cum, and when that moment came she dismounted. She grabbed him with her skinless hand and milked him close to her face. His semen shot into her mouth and the presence within her absorbed it, feasting on the beginnings of what could have been life.

Javier stepped forward and put the knife in her hand.

"Kill him," he said.

Behind her, The Goddess hummed with approval.

Rutger crawled across the floor.

Kandi watched him struggle to get his arm beneath the couch. She knew what he was going for. Luckily Javier was too busy to notice.

Jessica had the knife in her hands. The creature had moved up behind her and had wrapped all of its arms around her waist and chest while its legs ensnared her lower body. It had each of its heads on her shoulders and its breasts were pressed flat into her back, its penis cumming blood all over her ass. It pumped and flowed endlessly and ran down the insides of her legs.

Kandi wanted to help Toby, but, although he was the one in restraints, she too was immobilized. Not only was the wind and goo sticking her to the floor, her own fear had overpowered her, a fear she had not felt since she had been a child. She wanted to rise to her feet. She wanted to come to his aid. But she knew that if she dared move, she would find herself the next victim of these abominations.

She hoped Rutger could find the gun in time.

"Kill him!" Javier said again.

At first she thought his voice had echoed, but then she realized it was the flies. They bounced back the same demand to Jessica, their wings bending and clicking to form the words. The creature, without opening its mouths, said the same.

Kill him! Kill him! Kill him!

The chant surged around them along with the fire, making Kandi's heart drum like machine gun fire.

Jessica's face was demonic. The eyes blazed and the fangs dripped with drool.

She raised the blade over her head with both hands.

"Jessica!" Toby screamed. "Don't! *I love you*!"

Jessica froze and Kandi saw a hint of the girl's former face shine through. The jaw shrank slightly and the warped brow retreated. Her arms began to shiver.

"Listen to him, Jess!" Kandi shouted. "He came to take you with him, just like you knew he would! He wants you! He needs you! He always has!"

Javier turned toward Kandi.

"You bitch!" he said, and he came running at her.

Rutger popped out from behind the couch with the pistol that had fallen beneath it when he had first knocked Javier to the ground.

The gun fired again and again.

Javier seemed to dance as his body was jerked about. The bullets hit, some passing right through him while others got lodged inside his body. Rutger was a good shot. He managed to land several in Javier's chest, and as he spun around and fell, Rutger raised the barrel to the back of the man's head and sent his brains out the front of his face.

Watching this, Kandi saw a smile return to Jessica. The violence had pleased her and the dark forces were filling her up again with the cold, hard bloodlust.

"Snap out of it, Jessica!" Kandi said. "Toby loves you!"

"I do!" Toby said. "I love you, Jessica!"

Jessica looked to Kandi and then Toby. Her expression continued to change. One minute she was frothing and the next minute she was weeping, a confused mess of a girl.

The two-headed creature seemed to sense her reluctance. Its flesh became more yielding, like dough, and it began to roll over and around her, drawing her closer. Its stitches popped open as the dead flesh came alive. It groped her and began melding itself to her curves.

It was *absorbing* her.

Jessica began to shake, gurgling sounds coming from her throat.

Standing up, Rutger ran to them and put the barrel to the monster's female head and fired. The shot broke it open, sending thousands of flies soaring all around them, and the male head gasped, sucking air in a desperate cry. He screamed silently as the creature's body slunk off of Jessica and spun backward in the throes of agony.

Jessica, enraged, sent the knife into Rutger's neck. He screamed and dropped the gun as a jet of blood sprayed from the wound, dousing Toby. Jessica drew the knife out and began stabbing him again and again, sinking the blade into his chest, his shoulder, and his cheek. She grabbed the top of his head and slammed the knife through his eye, expunged it, and then slammed it into the other one and popped it out too.

Kandi forced herself to move and reach for the gun.

Rutger collapsed and Jessica crushed his eyes in her hand and returned her attention to Toby. The creature swam back to the ceiling and the army of bugs covered Jessica's entire body so that only her face could be seen. Her freckles faded in and out, twinkling just like the flies' bottoms.

Kandi grabbed the gun and looked around the room.

Ben was propped up behind his camera. He was either passed out from loss of blood or he was dead. She couldn't tell which. Mia had fallen to the floor. She had pissed herself and was babbling. The bugs were eating her face.

Jessica straddled Toby again and raised the knife.

Kandi fired.

Kandi knew she couldn't risk hitting Toby by shooting Jessica. She simply wasn't that good of a shot. So she decided to shoot the creature, knowing this would get Jessica's attention.

She unloaded on it, emptying the magazine. One after

another the bullets flew. She hit the body, one of the legs, and two arms. She landed a bullet in the already shattered head and then blasted the dick off. She tried to shoot the living, screaming head but it moved through the body, floating on its slime.

Jessica roared and the flames went higher. She got off of Toby and came at Kandi with the knife. But Kandi still held the gun and she flipped it over, grabbed the hot barrel, and knocked Jessica in the head with it. Jessica fell, the knife spinning away. Kandi climbed on top of her and pistol-whipped her once more.

"Wake up!" Kandi said. "You have to fight it!"

Jessica writhed beneath her in animal estrus—arms slashing, yellow teeth grinding, her red eyes bleeding as her whole head filled with throbbing veins. All Kandi could do was hit her again and again until the creature fell upon her from above.

Chapter Thirty-Nine

This one too, he thought.

This one shall be mine.

She destroyed Simone's face and Tiffany's lovely skull.

She will make a fine replacement.

Harold knew that she too had felt the divine touch of the red dust. The bloodlust had overtaken the one they called Kandi more than once, he knew. She had allowed it in the name of her art.

This woman can be one of us.

She just needs to know that she belongs and that she is loved.

He let his gelatinous form splash upon her in a blessing of sickness. His many fingers prodded her holes and his legs snaked around hers. But she didn't embrace his love. Instead she rejected him. Rejected him like so many others when he had been forced to live among them.

She screamed and bit at one of his hands.

She needs to be persuaded, just as Tiffany had.

The dust covered her and the flies made her a blinding tiara, but still she fought the urge. The power was welcoming her. It wanted her and it loved her. But she was stubborn and unappreciative.

The nerve of this movie slut.

Suddenly Harold felt her yield, just slightly, and let the bloodlust into her at last, if only a little bit. But she used it to rear back with the pistol and cracked him on the skull. Pain rocketed through him and his grip on her loosened, the magic of love ebbing from her sting.

Chapter Forty

Kandi pulled herself away from the thing's clutches and crawled to the table, ignoring her shattered kneecap. Behind her, Jessica was gathering herself and above them the creature was still reeling from the blow Kandi had delivered with the gun. She found the meat hook and hid it behind her back as she stood up, limping.

The creature was coming back for her.

Its remaining head had puckered lips as if readying for a kiss, and she could feel it leering despite its lack of eyes. Its lust for her was its weakness. It came closer and its arms opened to embrace her.

She let it get nice and close.

Kandi lunged with the hook, sending it into the creature's dark vagina, where it had already been shot. She dug and twisted its innards, enjoying its screams. With her other hand she grabbed an arm and pulled the creature lower. She forced the hook up further, shredding open the stomach. Cold guts spewed forth, reeking of wet rot and swimming with glowing maggots. She pushed higher and higher as the creature wailed. Elbow-deep in the creature's meat chasm, black blood covered her.

The bloodlust exploded within Kandi.

Thunder boomed and fire crackled.

The foul stink of death gagged her, but she kept on pressing, letting the fury fuel her just enough so that she could stay alive.

Finally, the hook hit something hard. A muscle.

The heart.

She pierced it and twisted.

The stitches on the limbs began to snap and the staples popped and flew into the fire. The limbs flailed as they unraveled from the torso. An arm fell and then two legs, then the mangled crotch plummeted like a guillotine blade. Kandi stepped back and the creature fell to the floor, spewing as it started falling apart.

Jessica tackled her and they rolled in the blood.

"No!" Toby yelled. "Jessica, please, *no*!"

They were fighting at his feet and Jessica was winning. She ripped out a large chunk of Kandi's hair and clawed at her breasts. She sliced her flesh with the claw-like nails and the spittle that sprayed from her mouth scalded Kandi's shoulder like boiling water. She swung at Jessica with her fists, connecting but doing no apparent damage.

"You heathen!" Jessica said. "You have no respect for art!"

Kandi felt the knife stab into her side. Jessica dropped it and pinned Kandi by the throat with one hand and started digging at her fresh wound with the other. She felt Jessica's fingers begin to curl into her body as she hissed.

"Such loveliness," Jessica said. "A body built for the pleasures of the flesh."

Jessica was choking her. Kandi kicked and shook. She pounded Jessica's arm, but it wouldn't budge. She was getting woozy, her eyes glazing with stars.

Toby rocked his chair forward. "No!"

He fell into Jessica and his weight pushed her off of Kandi. Jessica was stunned for the moment, and Kandi tried to catch her breath. She got up on her elbows, saw the knife, and went for it. She was about to cut at Toby's ropes, but then she spotted the handcuffs.

Fuck!

It didn't matter anyway. The veins in Jessica's head had swelled beyond her skin and tears of blood poured from the corners of her eyes.

Kandi moved forward with caution, the knife out with both hands.

Pain ravaged her. Her side burned as it poured blood down her leg.

So much blood. It's everywhere.

Jessica wobbled on her feet and her breasts rose and fell. She was breathing hard and fast now. Her hands went to her head.

"*The pressure . . .*" she said. "*It is awakening . . .*"

Jessica's veins were purple, but Kandi could see the pulsing red dots swimming within them, the little flies swimming through her mind, carrying whatever dark presence had made a home in her soul.

"I can't take it," Jessica said. "I'm not strong enough. I cannot be *The Goddess*."

"Let it go, Jessica," Kandi said. "*Let it go*! You don't want this in your soul!"

"Oh, God. *It hurts . . .*"

But she still kept walking.

Not sure if it was a trick, Kandi raised the knife and took a step back.

"Toby?" Jessica said.

He lay on his side. His head had hit the floor hard and a small lump was now bleeding. "I'm here, Jessica."

Jessica got down on her knees to see him better.

"It really *is* you," she said.

"Of course it is," he said. "I came back for you."

"You did?"

"I couldn't leave you, baby. Not here and not in Humboldt. I couldn't leave you behind. Not for anything. I love you."

Now Jessica cried real tears, clear and pure. Kandi was still dizzy, but it looked to her like Jessica's eyes had lightened from red into a softer pink.

"You *love* me?" Jessica said.

"Yeah, baby. I'm not going to leave you behind."

She ran her hand through his hair and they both cried.

"But, baby," she said. "*I'm already gone.*"

Kandi tensed, thinking Jessica might attack him, but she just kept on petting.

"I'm already gone, Toby. I'm already gone."

The fire was everywhere now. The house was engulfed in it and black smoke was filling up the room. With the creature dead, the cyclone of ooze had fallen into the pile of burnt goop on the floor, but the flies still swarmed.

Jessica slipped one of her yellowed nails beneath Toby's ropes and cut them away in one slash. She took his cuffs and effortlessly snapped them in half at the chain. Then she tore away the restraints at his feet and slid the chair from under him. Toby got up slowly, watching Jessica. Neither he nor Kandi knew what to expect now. There seemed to be a change in Jessica, but they both knew that violence and death were very real threats, as was the demon of the flies within her.

We have to get out of here, Kandi thought.

"Then go," Jessica said.

There was no sense in trying to trick her or sneak away now. She was in their minds.

"Go," Jessica said.

Kandi lowered her arms, but she wouldn't drop the knife. She looked to Ben and saw that his body was on fire. He was still limp, propped up in his chair behind the camera. On the floor in front of him, Mia was curled into a ball. The insects had devoured her exposed skin, leaving her head as a skull with hair. Her skeletal hands had dug into the floor so hard that they were lodged into the hard wood.

Kandi leaned into Toby. He was shaking hard and was

sobbing now. She put her arm around his shoulder and started to limp forward.

"Come on," she said.

Jessica did not watch them. She reached her arms out as if crucified and the flies whirled around her, bringing the flames with them.

"No," Toby cried. "No!"

But Jessica was right. It was too late.

Far, far too late.

Chapter Forty-One

They jumped through one of the shattered windows, making a quick leap over the flames that framed it. Each of them cried out in their pain, but the rain felt good. It washed away the blood and slime from Kandi's naked body and it cleansed her of the bugs and ash. The lightning flashed and made white veins through the dark sky. She tried to shake the thought of Jessica's exposed veins from her mind.

The sudden flash lit up the ranch and she saw the small, fuzzy shape of a cat sprinting across the lawn and away from the inferno. She and Toby took Cougar's lead and ran through the yard too, getting as far away from the house as possible. The flames were climbing higher now, devouring Malone Manor. A plume of red dust shrouded the house, and as the roof collapsed thousands upon thousands of the gleaming flies rose up in a single jet and spun into the blackness. Lightning cracked the sky and the flies followed the bolts into the darkness, making red snakes against the flashing clouds.

Together they created a deafening drone.

Spooked, the horses ran to the fence, braying and kicking at the bars in an effort to escape.

"We have to get out," Kandi said. "How do we open the gate?"

"We can't."

"What?"

"It's locked from the inside."

"No!"

Tears of panic filled her eyes.

"Don't worry," he said. "Just follow me."

Toby held the ladder for Kandi as she climbed. She waited for him there, straddling the fence. He had given her his t-shirt to cover herself and she clutched it to her, hugging her body as she swayed. It was already drenched.

Toby began to climb up the rungs, and as he reached the midway point, he looked over his shoulder at the blazing inferno the mansion had become. The bulk of the swarm had sailed away into the sky and the red dust had dissipated. All there was now was the thick smoke and the devouring, raging flames.

A lump filled his throat. He hadn't been lying to Jessica.

He didn't want to leave her.

He did love her.

He made his way up to the top of the fence and pulled the ladder over to the other side. As Kandi climbed down Toby took one last look at the imploding house, and through the open side window, through the wall of flame, he could make out a single dark shape. It was a woman's silhouette, walking through the smoke, engulfed in flames.

She raised one arm, waved at him, and then splintered into hundreds of flies that flew up and out of the window, sailing free, lost forever in the gentle gust of the warm, night wind.

Epilogue

Only one person sent Vic discs anymore. But that man was dead. The fire had left nothing but ashes and a few charred bones so warped they were impossible to identify. Rutger Malone, the once famous porno director who made underground movies for Vic's special clientele, had been one of many to die in the house fire. And the special film he'd been making had been destroyed with him.

Vic turned the disc over in his hand. There was nothing written on it, just a red-hued disc that arrived in the mail. The envelope it came in was coated in a light red dust, as if it had traveled across the desert to find him. There was no note inside and no return address, but the route of the postal stamp revealed it had come from Tennessee.

Rutger's house had been in the Great Smokey Mountains.

Vic walked through his spacious living room, his silk robe fluttering in the breeze of the air conditioning, cranked to combat the cruelty of summer in Nevada. He sipped his morning espresso as he headed to his home office.

Maybe it's the dailies I'd asked for. Rutger never liked to show unfinished work, but, as the producer, Victor Crews had demanded at least a taste of the work-in-progress. It was supposed to be his most depraved film yet, if not the most depraved film ever made. Based on the quality of Vic's other productions, the upcoming Rutger Malone feature had been pre-ordered by hundreds of customers through their dark web site, all of which Vic had to refund to keep their business after the fire effectively canceled the movie. It was a financial loss, seeing how he'd put up a good deal of money for classic porn star Kandi Hart to appear in the film, but it was a knuckle he just had to bite.

Kandi was one of only two people who had escaped death the night the house went up in flames. He'd considered getting some of his heavies to bring her in for questioning, but the woman's mental state was so deteriorated, Vic figured he'd be wasting his time. Worse than that, he'd be wasting more moneyHis latest film was gone for good . . . or so he'd thought.

If there's anything *I can use on this, even just twenty minutes of dismemberment erotica, abuse porn, bloodlettings, flesh-eating—anything up to hardcore standards—I can release a short film and recoup some losses.*

He sat down at his desktop, facing his grayed reflection in the screen. An older Mac, still having a disc drive, awoke from its sleep, and Vic inserted the disc. He bit at his thumbnail as the data loaded, silently praying to see the ultimate of sins. A file appeared on the screen.

Goddesses—a film by Rutger Malone.

Vic wet his lips.

The video file opened, the movie filling the screen. There was no opening credit sequence. The film just started off in a sterile-looking room. A man was having his arm sawed off while Kandi Hart masturbated. He was spraying semen, blissed out on his own amputation. Vic, now in his late fifties, often suffered erectile dysfunction, but he grew instantly and totally hard, as thrilled by the derangement he was watching as he was by the knowledge he now possessed Rutger Malone's final, twisted opus. Judging by this opening sequence, it was a real doozy. Vic could make his money back and then some.

A line of red static blipped across the screen. It seemed odd to have a glitch considering the quality of equipment they'd used. Vic ignored it. A minor imperfection, inconsequential to the overall effect. But then there was another. And another. Vic stirred. The static grew thicker, a red haze layering itself over the images.

"Christ on the cross," he muttered.

He waited, hoping it would smooth out. That's when he realized another image was forming, something superimposed over the action. A humanoid shape bloomed out of that crackling, crimson static. Vic leaned in, making out the upper body of a young woman. She was naked, her red hair dripping with what appeared to be blood. Her pale skin pulsated with freckles that swarmed across her flesh like fire ants.

She had perfect breasts, but one of her nipples had been torn off. And unlike the images she was imposed over, the redhead was not part of the action. She was not engaged in anything other than staring straight at the camera, through the computer screen, and directly into Victor Crews's eyes. Her stare made his bones ache. His chest went tight, limbs numb. The young lady before him was a glittering demon, as alluring as she was inexplicably horrific, making his balls draw tight and blood run cold. When she smiled—directly at him—a small cry escaped Vic, and even before the red dust began to seep from the slit of the disc drive, he knew he was being taken in the most paralyzing way.

The dust pulsed through the room. Then came the insects, flickering in the air like homing beacons, guiding him somewhere more perverse than the human atrocities involved in his most heinous of crimes. On screen, the young woman raised one hand. Her arm was skinned down to the elbow, the sinew flapping on the bone in sopping chunks. She brought the ruined hand to her lips and blew Vic a kiss. He smiled, knowing he was hers now, all he was and all he had.

Hers alone. Forever in the thrall of The Goddess.

THE DEVOURING

"THE FIRST TIME I had sex," she said, "I was nineteen."

"That's not too scandalous."

"Well," she admitted, coyly, her faint British accent adding to her exoticism, "it was with *me* Uncle."

Violet had insisted that a game of truth or dare could show people whether they would be compatible or not on a first date, as long as the game was straightforward. So we'd started with a few truths. She'd asked me intense questions: what my most painful memory was, who was the most prominent person in my masturbation fantasies, if I was to murder someone which weapon would I use? I had answered as honestly as I could: losing my mother, Madeline Smith, and a hatchet. She didn't ask for explanations, just answers. My questions to her had been timid at first, but given the nature of her own questions, I'd decided that I shouldn't bore her, so I asked about her first sexual experience and now she'd answered.

"He'd always eyed me," she said, "and there was a manliness to him that I'd never found in the boys at school. It wasn't rape. In fact, I advanced on him."

I didn't know how to respond.

"Now it's my turn," she said. "Truth or dare?"

"Truth," I said, though I was curious about a dare.

"How'd you lose your finger?"

I looked down at my left hand. Only half of the pinkie was there, severed at the knuckle.

"Dare," I said.

She didn't object to the change, but I could sense the curiosity the secrecy gave her. It spun in her wide eyes and curled in the corners of her mouth.

"Close your eyes," she said.

"Is that the whole dare?"

"Close them and let me show you something."

I did and felt her scoot closer to me on the couch. She breathed into my ear. I thought at first that she was going to kiss me, being as forward as she was, but instead she licked my earlobe. I soon felt her head resting in my lap. She made no effort to undo my slacks, but she found the bulge of my erection and put her mouth on the shaft. She bit it. Not hard or fiercely, but enough to apply pressure. Good, sweet pain. She held me there in her jaws for a moment, like a dog with a rubber newspaper. Then she released me and sat up.

"You like that?" she asked.

"Yes, I did."

"So did *me* uncle."

This was the nature of Violet, the Violet I grew to know. But I think I've gotten ahead of myself with this. For, to truly understand Violet, and myself for that matter, I should explain how we came to meet.

"You have a nice collection," she said, gazing through my boxes of imports, out-of-prints and rare bootlegs.

I'd seen her wandering about that afternoon at HorrorCon, a convention for horror enthusiasts. I made a living with obscure DVD sales. While not everyone is interested in films like *Subconscious Cruelty, Meet the Feebles, Santa Sangre,* or *Invasion of the Blood Farmers*, there is a minority out there that hungers for such gore-smeared flicks.

She'd been noticed by just about everyone there. She was tall but wore high heels anyway, accentuating her unusual height. Her dress inflamed the senses as it molded to her body like wet tissue, her nipples revealed in the chill. Her hair was so blonde it looked nearly white, and it framed her pallor face like a sickle. But it was her eyes that stunned me most; her harrowing eyes. They reminded me of Barbara Steele's in Bava's classic *Black Sunday*; wide and possessed.

"Well, well," she said, coyly, holding up a DVD. "*Antropophagus?*"

"Indeed," I replied, "the 1980 classic."

"I was disappointed with *The Grim Reaper*. What a rip-off."

A little known fact in the fanboy world is that the film *Antropophagus* was released on DVD in America with the alternate title *The Grim Reaper*. The film was also edited to pieces, eliminating all of the grisly scenes which gave it its notoriety, including the infamous scene where a fetus is expunged from a pregnant mother and consumed, as well as my personal favorite part: the finale of self-cannibalism.

"My inventory is entirely censorship free," I told her.

"I lived in England during the madness over all the video nasties, when Thatcher's censorship was in full bloom. As a teen getting to see a bootlegged copy of *The Last House on the Left* was just about the most exciting thing in the world."

"I read about that—"

"Any porno?"

She was looking dead at me with those eyes, menacing like Medusa's before her head-snakes turned men to stone.

"Not here, just soft-core horror stuff. Misty Mundane, that sort of thing."

"How droll."

"Vampire erotica not your thing?"

"Well, the oldies are not without their charm. Lena Lomay writhing around naked for an hour and a half, dyking out and drinking blood. But these new soft-core, goth pictures are such a bore. The sex is fake and the horror elements are gormless kitsch. I mean, do me a favor."

"You prefer something more intense?"

"Internet's the way to go, but you have to be careful."

"Yeah, there's a lot of sickos out there."

"It's not the crazies I worry about, it's the filth . . . by which I mean the police. So many rules and regulations. So many people monitoring what you look at. It's bloody intrusive."

I wondered just what sort of porn sparked her interest. I remained timid on the outside, even though my insides pulsed. And so it was she who led me.

"I like some of the real dirt," she said. "Humiliation, consensual torture."

I swallowed heavily at the reality of her being like my most filthy dream made flesh.

"People frown on it all though," she said, "just as they frown on all these bloody pictures of yours. But really, what's the problem with a rape fantasy, as long as it's fantasy, right?"

To my joy she'd accepted my invitation to the screening of *Doorway to Goreday* and I'd gone to her apartment to pick her up. We'd engaged in our round of truth or dare, where her quick nibbling of my cock was as far as we'd gone physically, but psychologically we had expunged much from one another's exposed souls.

After the film we went to a late diner where our conversation escalated.

"What's the most intense film you've seen?" she asked.

"That depends."

"Come off it. In your line of work? There must be one that stands out at the forefront of your head."

She was right of course. I had immediately thought of the forty minute short entitled *Bloody Bathroom*. I'd only received a copy under the most secretive of circumstances. I'd never shown it to anyone or spoken of it in a manner that might suggest that I had a VHS copy stashed away in my safe at home.

"It really depends. *Faces of Death* contains real animal deaths and fake human deaths. The Japanese *Guinea Pig* series is splendidly brutal, as is the *Angel Guts* rape-movie series. *Cannibal Holocaust—*"

"About a week ago I saw a real pisser," she interrupted. "Two blokes pussy-pound this silly cunt for twenty minutes. They spank her arse with belts making it glow like Christmas. Then they tie her to the end of the bed. The one bloke fucks her mouth till she's choking and her mascara is running from tears."

At this point, Violet laughed as she reflected.

"Then," she continued, "they pull out this vice. They put it into her mouth and it forces her mouth to stay open, the brackets pushing her jaw down as far as it will go. Then they start jerking themselves in her face, and it's funny cause it reminded me of that carny game with the water pistols and the clown heads, cause then they shot their fun all over her face, trying to get as much of it in her mouth as possible, like it was a contest."

She laughed heartily.

"That was a bloody good show," she said, "but I've seen better. You've seen better too, I'm sure."

Back at my place, an hour later, we sat watching rare documentary footage shot in Polynesia. The footage was of tribes preparing human flesh for ritual cannibalism. Violet was engrossed in these images that I had viewed numerous times. But I was still excited by the real-life devouring of people by people. When we came to the footage of the Binderwurs of central India consuming the severed limbs of their dead, Violet spread out upon the couch with her legs toward me. Her bare feet dug into my crotch. She separated her knees and slid her skirt up around her waist. She wore no panties and was freshly shaven. The flesh of her legs was even paler than the doll-like skin of her face, but here, on her inner thighs, the flesh was covered in razor scars. She placed her hand on the back of my neck and pulled my head down into the moist, warm welcoming darkness of her opening.

Her eyes never left the screen.

It was then that I knew I was falling in love with her.

The belt was tight enough around her neck to give her the full effect of throttling. Her face was pink and growing redder, heading toward the bliss. She lay on her stomach on the bed, and I straddled her, my erection buried deep inside her. On the television, a bad bondage porno played. We were now one week into our relationship and the passion was psychotic; a bloodlust-fueled marathon of sexual mania.

As her eyes rolled into her skull, she passed out and I came.

I loosened the belt and pulled out. I rolled her over and immediately tended to her with the smelling salts, snapping her awake in seconds. Drool fell from her swollen lips as she gasped, her breasts heaving as her lungs went into overdrive.

"Darling," she said once her breathing steadied, "that's the fuck I've been gagging for."

She turned her head towards the flicker of the screen. An old woman was smacking a redhead's ass.

"What a waste this is," Violet complained. "This old tart whipping this silly twit."

I exited the bathroom, my eyes on the safe in the corner. By now we'd ventured into some truly taboo places. We'd beaten and bruised each other and when it had brought us to the edge of suffering we'd pushed on. She'd given me almost as much as I'd ever dreamed. I figured I shouldn't hold out on her.

"I have a present for you," I said.

Her eyes seemed to glow with anticipation even though I'd never told her about the movie. Somehow she just knew what was coming, and that she had earned the viewing.

"I must have been a very good girl," she said as I opened up the safe and pulled out the cassette.

"Better," I corrected, "you've been a very bad one."

I scooted back onto the bed and we got comfortable. She clung to me in a combination of heightened excitement, sexual tension, and even a little bit of fear. The screen faded in. The words *Bloody Bathroom* were written on a page in marker. The paper was lowered, revealing a filthy bathroom. A man came on screen, nude except for a pair of boots, rubber gloves, and a leather gimp mask with motorcycle goggles covering his eyes. He grunted and two other men came on screen in similar dress, but one was boney and hairless with yellowish skin and the other was muscular and well hung. They carried a medical examiner's body bag that was writhing. Muted screams came from within it.

I felt Violet's hand close around my arm.

We watched as the fat man ordered the others to lower the bag. The boney man ran toward the camera and picked it up, zooming in on it. It was unzipped to reveal a young woman with a ball gag in her mouth. There was no mistaking the fear in her face. This was real. The man pulled her out of the bag and dropped her onto the floor. She was bound and unable to break her fall. She was already nude and the men went to work on her, raping her for the next twenty minutes; degrading her, beating her and torturing her in the most vile ways fathomable.

Violet watched it, silent and enthralled.

She flinched when the fat man went off screen only to come back with a butcher knife. The muscular man was sodomizing the victim at this point. He quickly finished and spun her over for the facial. The fat man held her head for him, and as he climaxed the fat man began stabbing her.

Violet gasped and we watched the second half of the film. It was a bloodbath of violent snuff. The victim was killed and eviscerated while the villains played with her insides. The screen went black and the tape abruptly ended.

As always, the film left me with the same mixed feelings of terror and shamefully joyous voyeurism. But I was curious about how Violet felt. She'd been quiet throughout the picture, never objecting, never turning away. But I had not been able to see her face. Her head had been resting on my chest.

With the film over, the room fell black.

"My god," she whispered. "It was brilliant."

She went into the bathroom and vomited.

"There's many different forms of fame, Alex," she said the next day. "You have the mega-fame: the movie stars and T.V. cunts. But then there's the glory of underground fame; the names whispered in darkest corners. Names like *Bloody Bathroom*."

"You really think its art?"

"It's bloody trash, it's vile and wrong, but its art nonetheless. It affected me more deeply than anything I've ever seen."

"It's just shock value though, cause it's real."

"It's more than that, Alex. It's not just sick curiosity or even subconscious sadism. It's the hunger for stimulation; the endless desire for the new and bold. It's not just the rape and the gore and the reality of it all. It's easy to understand that there is a small group of loonies out there who do this sort of thing. The brilliance of it is that people who don't do this sort of thing, who wouldn't ever have the balls to or perhaps not even the desire to, still want to see it. Whether people admit it or not there is a side to everyone that wants to witness things that are almost impossible to imagine, let alone see. The genius of snuff is not its existence but rather its universal appeal. While totally repugnant, it is still more enticing than the filthiest porn."

"I suppose your right there."

"It's a more wonderful form of praise, isn't it? All those

Hollywood cunts make these shitbaths of pictures. They make trophies for each other and it's all just a good show. But on the streets, on the lips of every one, pervert or priest, are the names of the nasties, the bloody snuffs. That's fuckin' glory there."

We were at her apartment, in the shower so we wouldn't get blood on her bed sheets. I'd punctured her neck and I was feasting on her like a vampire while she caressed my testicles, sinking her nails into the sack. I was using her favorite of my fingers on her: the nub.

"Truth," I said, her blood on my lips.

She opened her eyes, confused.

"What's that then?"

"Truth," I repeated, giving her a telling stare.

Now she understood. She knew the question we'd left off on, back when our relationship was just starting.

"Right then," she moaned, "how'd you lose the finger?"

"I chopped it off with a hatchet."

She began grinding her pelvis into my hand.

"You see," I continued, "there are all kinds of fetishes. I'd heard about one that makes it so some people can't have an orgasm unless something is being amputated. I don't have this problem, as you well know. But I was curious about the condition."

"So you went for it. That's so ballsy, baby."

"That's not the whole story," I said. "It took a lot for me to build up the nerve to do it. But I was alone. I had no sexual partner for months. My movies and my masturbation were all I had. You already know about my boyhood fixation on Madeline Smith."

"Oh yes, the Bond-girl."

"Right," I said. "Well, my obsession with her never left me, only escalated. During those lonely months, I grew sick over her. I pulled a Van Gogh, you might say. I chopped off the finger as a tribute. I'd planned to mail it to her for Valentine's Day."

"Did you?"

"No."

"But why?" she asked as if heartbroken.

"After the excitement of hacking it off, I began to think more clearly. Most women would panic if they received a finger in the mail. The police would be notified. It might all lead back to me."

"So do you still have the finger?"

"Well, I knew I couldn't preserve it for long, and I was too embarrassed by the idea of rushing to the emergency room to have it reattached. Besides, it had been a profound moment in my life and I wanted it to stay severed, the nub being a reminder of the madness I'd reached. But I didn't want to just toss the finger. I wanted to keep it, but not frozen or something stupid like that. So, that night, I ate it."

For a moment we both fell silent. She stared at me.

"What was it like to do that?"

"While I felt like I'd hit rock bottom, at the same time I felt liberated."

"Just like watching snuff."

"Exactly, only better because I was involved."

We fell silent again as she stared at me with those animal eyes. It was then that I realized that she had fallen in love with me as well.

"Alex, darling."

"Yes?"

"I want to make a movie with you."

We watched the video together while she soaked her foot in ice. She'd taken a few painkillers and was doing fine. The video had come out good, Violet doing an excellent job filming, her hand not even shaking much as I'd severed her toe, even though she screamed. Watching myself eat it made me feel about the same as I'd felt earlier while actually eating it. I was into it, but it wasn't the same as when I had eaten my finger. Something was lacking, flaccid.

"We're off to a great start," Violet said. "But it needs more. A little cannibalism goes a long way, but we need to get things in perspective."

"I've been trying to come up with ideas but nothing's struck me, you know? Rape, torture, murder; it's all been done."

We sat there thinking as we watched. And just like that, something came to me.

"You've given a toe," I said. "Now it's my turn."

"Alright, but no more toes," she said, "we don't want to be redundant."

From my point of view, I filmed her on her knees before me, performing fellatio. We got typically kinky with it, the deep-throating and cheek smacking. Then up came the dagger. She teased me, scraping the shaft. Then she ever so slowly began to cut away a small section of my erection's flesh, not anything like a castration, just shaving a section of skin. She did this and then began sucking on it in a frenzy before chewing the striped flesh.

I exploded in her face as she ate me, and it was the most intense orgasm of my life.

I knew then what had been missing when I had devoured her toe. It wasn't so much the eating of human flesh that excited me: *it was having my own flesh eaten*. Eating myself was nauseating bliss, but being devoured by a beautiful woman was the sweetest fetish of all.

And Valentine's Day was drawing nearer.

After I'd been bandaged and we'd watched the tape with fervor, I told Violet my epiphany of the ultimate gesture of love.

"Snuff is redundant because it's all murder," I said. "What if, instead of a victim, there was a willing participant?"

"Holy hell," she said. "It's perfect."

"It would add levels of depravity, horror and fetishism the likes of which the world has never seen. Think of it: a film where someone willingly dies, and even enjoys it. Better yet, instead of a pretty woman being snuffed by insane men, we have an insane man being snuffed by a pretty woman. The man is not just killed, but eaten alive. Not just by the woman, but by himself too."

Strapped now to the slab, I lay beneath Violet who rides me, films me, shreds me. The agony and ecstasy are one, an insufferable heaven. I am in thrall, but my most erotic nightmare has come true, so I am free. The feel of her fingers twisting in my abdomen is as wonderful as the feeling of my erection that now spews inside her. This is the masterpiece we give to the world, our blessing of sickness bestowed upon the already infected.

Violet has agreed with my final wishes and is going to complete the film on her own. The porno-snuff footage we've shot will be put together in a montage of our best moments, then the film will build up to this scene where I am willingly eaten alive. The remainder of the film will then be of Violet first having whatever sex she can with my corpse, then a thorough dismemberment, then the cooking and eating of my remains. She will then edit a rough final cut and send free copies to all of the people I have listed on my hard drive, my records of all the customers I've had for my horror and porno films: the nasties. Once completed, close to a thousand people will have an authentic snuff film, and as anyone in the underground film business knows, the circulation won't stop there.

Violet's face appears on the film, and I've suggested she blur it, but she's insisted on leaving it in for the integrity of the film. She doesn't care if its release might put her in prison. The trial would see more exposure than the O.J.

Simpson case. It would all just hype the movie up even more.

I can feel death tightening as Violet pushes my intestines into my mouth. As everything goes black, I taste a flavor that is the true so-called nectar of the gods; I chew with what little energy I have left.

She bends down and her mouth drips blood as she whispers into my ear: “I love you, darling. Happy Valentine’s Day.”

This is the proudest achievement of our lives.

This is the outcome of our desires.

This is the very pinnacle of our art.

ACKNOWLEDGMENTS

Thanks to Marc Ciccarone and everyone at Blood Bound Books for daring to release my most depraved work to date, and for dedicating themselves to this fever dream of a project with such gusto.

Appreciations to my beta-reader and book buddy, Nicole Amburgey. Thanks to Creston Hannaford and Gregg Kirby for their invaluable friendship and for always joining me in watching some of the most lowdown, grotesque, and cheese-filled trash cinema imaginable. Appreciations to all of my fans and supporters, as well as all of my writer and editor friends.

Big thanks to Thomas Mumme, always.

And special thanks to Lindsay Lohan for being a continued source of inspiration.

About the Author

Kristopher Triana is the Splatterpunk Award-winning author of *Full Brutal, Gone to See the River Man, Blood Relations, Body Art* and many other terrifying books. He is also the author of the crime thrillers *The Ruin Season* and *Shepherd of the Black Sheep*. His work has been published in multiple languages and has drawn praise from the likes of Publisher's Weekly, *Rue Morgue Magazine, Cemetery Dance, Scream Magazine, The Horror Fiction Review* and many more.

He is also the co-host of the podcast *Vital Social Issues 'N Stuff with Kris and John Wayne.*

He lives somewhere in New England.

Visit him at: Kristophertriana.com
Twitter: Koyotekris
Facebook: Kristopher Triana
Instagram: Kristopher_Triana
Podcast: krisandjohnwayne.com

Made in the USA
Las Vegas, NV
03 August 2022

52625197R00156